# THE PYRAMID
# DECEPTION
## by
# AUSTIN S.
# CAMACHO

ISBN 978-1-940758-06-0

Cover Design by instinctivedesign

Published by:
Intrigue Publishing
11505 Cherry Tree Crossing RD #148
Cheltenham, MD 20623-9998

Printed in the United States of America

Also by Austin S. Camacho

**The Hannibal Jones Mysteries**

The Troubleshooter
Blood and Bone
Collateral Damage
Damaged Goods
Russian Roulette

**The Stark and O'Brien Adventures**

The Payback Assignment
The Orion Assignment
The Piranha Assignment
The Ice Woman Assignment

**Stand Alone Thriller**

Beyond Blue

# THE PYRAMID DECEPTION

-1-

# Wednesday

Was the woman he loved really trying to kill herself?

Hannibal had to consider the possibility. Cindy Santiago had apologized for taking the phone call in the middle of their rare mid-week lunch together. At first she tried to make the news seem unimportant, but he was, after all, a detective. He had seen the breath catch in her throat. He had watched her smooth, Latin face segue from stunned to angry to lost during the short conversation. He noted her careful choice of words, as if trying to conceal the topic of their meaning. And afterward, she was looking across the table toward him, but he doubted she was seeing him.

"Cindy?"

Her hand appeared to go numb, her phone slipping from her fingers. The phone made a cold, plastic noise as it bounced off the table. Her lips quivered without sound. She stood up, letting her napkin tumble silently to the floor. Her blank eyes moved side to side, searching.

"Cindy?"

She stepped toward the door and he rose to follow, grabbing his Oakleys but ignoring her phone and purse. Their things were safe in Rockland's, although he hated to abandon his barbecue. But DC lawyers never abandon their IPhones. For them it was like pulling a scuba diver's air hose loose. His girl looked dazed or in shock and he wasn't about to let her just wander away.

Outside, the sun burned through the thin strands of cotton candy clouds and Hannibal's eyes needed a second to adjust before he slid his sunglasses into place. When he pulled the world into focus, he saw Cindy standing between two parked cars about to step into the midday traffic pouring down Wisconsin Avenue.

A black Cadillac Escalade was bearing down on the spot she would step into. The driver was chatting on her phone, maintaining a paper-thin margin between her vehicle and the parked cars, trying to beat the light about to turn red on the corner. Cindy would be invisible to her until too late. A strangled cry jammed in Hannibal's throat. His right arm shot forward. He made eye contact with the driver, even as he clamped onto a handful of Cindy's shoulder-length hair and yanked back hard. A few auburn strands popped. Tires squealed just as the spiked heel of her left pump was about to touch asphalt. Then her back arched and her left foot flew upward. The Escalade jerked to a halt before she fell back into Hannibal's arms.

Before falling backward onto the sidewalk Hannibal saw her right shoe bounce off the Cadillac's grille. Had he pulled her so hard it flew off? Or had the Escalade really knocked the shoe off her foot? He would never know how close she came to death, and it was not the most important question of the day, anyway. He twisted her in his arms so he could see her face.

"What the hell is the matter with you? You could have been killed."

"Hannibal, it's all gone," Cindy said, her eyes welling up. "A fortune, all the money I had made, my entire savings, everything I've worked so hard for, it's all evaporated in a day."

## -2-

Hannibal handed Cindy her missing shoe and shoved her into his Volvo before running back to the restaurant for her phone and purse. The drive was not pleasant.

"Have you lost your mind?" Hannibal snapped as he pulled into traffic. "Were you trying to get yourself killed? And what the hell does that mean, it's all gone?"

Cindy seemed to be on the verge of hyperventilating during the drive. Hannibal thought back to their lunch, when they were planning a vacation on the Riviera to celebrate her recent good fortune. She had been able to cash in on a business offering she set up, and become an instant millionaire three times over thanks to the value of her stock options. Even after taxes that left a handsome sum. He was of course very proud of her because she earned her fortune through her own business and legal expertise, but he could not deny a certain discomfort in having his woman pay for their vacation.

Hannibal's modest flat wasn't exactly nearby but it was easier to drive to than Cindy's townhouse in Alexandria.

By the time he had her seated in his living room she was calm—or numb. She still sat with her single shoe in her lap, where she had carried it during the ride down to Southeast DC. Now she lifted it and waved it at him.

"This was a $300 dollar pair of Via Spiga pumps," she said, dropping the shoe on the floor.

Hannibal used his French press to brew two quick cups of coffee and set them on the coffee table as he settled on the sofa beside her. She showed her first smile since the phone call when she lifted her cup to her mouth.

"That smells so good. Thank you, lover."

Hannibal tasted his own coffee and waited. In a lifetime as a police detective, secret service agent and now a private detective he had learned that victims are more likely to tell you what you needed to know if you leave them some silence to fill. He savored the rich, hearty flavor of the exotic Costa Rican beans and watched her fawn colored eyes. After a moment, Cindy looked over as if a surprising thought had wandered into her mind.

"You're waiting for me, aren't you?" she asked. "You're sitting there, waiting for me to tell you why I'm so upset. You want to help me. I'm a client now, aren't I?"

"Is that the only way I can help you?" Hannibal asked, leaning toward her. "Can't I just be worried about my woman and want to help her?"

"But you're the world famous Troubleshooter," she said, moving from a defensive stance to offense. "This is what you do. You bail out losers."

Hannibal let the better part of a minute pass before he spoke again, and did so in a very soft tone. Her left foot was curled under her. He rested a hand on her left knee.

"Losers? Baby, you're a successful attorney at ground zero of lawyer central, earning a fat salary. Then you get a phone call and life suddenly seems to lose its meaning. What do I have to do to find out why?"

"It won't matter much," she said, turning away. "Even you can't fix this. It's my own fault, and there's nothing anybody can do about it. I'm afraid our vacation is off, Hannibal. I've lost the house, I've lost my savings, and I'm back to square one. Overnight I've lost everything."

As eager as Hannibal was to hold Cindy, he knew this was not the right time. In some ways this was not the woman who had come to his home so many times before. He was seeing things he had never seen in her before. Hopelessness. Depression. And now bitterness. In some ways, he would have to treat her like a client to help, but one way or another he had to take care of the woman he loved.

"All right, you're talking about the money you made off that big offering for a client, right?"

Cindy nodded.

"I know it was a big chunk of change, and I know you committed to a million-plus dollar house on the edge of Georgetown just a couple of days ago." The house that would redefine her success, he thought. The money that placed her suddenly so far above his modest income as an inner-city private investigator.

"Hannibal I fell in love with that house, and now I don't even have the down payment."

"Cindy, I know you loved the house. What I don't know is how you lost the money or why you think it was your fault."

"Because I invested it all in one place, looking for one big score to double my money. And it turned out to be a big scam." Her fists were clenched tight, and the edge on her voice was meant to cut her, not him. Behind the self-loathing Hannibal realized for the first time how much of his girl's self-esteem was tied up in her net worth. As much as he loved her, as well as he knew her, he wondered why he had never seen that before.

"Okay, it sounds like you went for an investment scheme of some kind," Hannibal said, keeping his voice gentle. "Some of the sharpest businessmen alive have made that kind of mistake. Was that your accountant who called you at lunch?"

Cindy's face clenched as if he had hit her in the gut. "No, that wasn't my accountant. This was all against his advice. That was Jason."

"Jason Moore?" Hannibal asked. "The other lawyer they hired when they got you? Drank a little too much at your birthday bash? You've always talked about him like a friend."

"He is," Cindy said. "Jason is my best friend in the world. Well, best male friend. You know how hard it is for a woman to be just friends with a man."

Hannibal didn't believe that, but knew a lot of women who did. Seeing them together, he knew for sure that their relationship was just that: close, solid friends. "You've known him longer than you've known me, right?"

"We've been back to back since I got to the firm, him doing tax law while I focused on the business law side. He's a good man and he knows his stuff. That's why I trusted him when he brought me this opportunity. It just seemed too good to pass up."

"So, he called to tell you he suspected a problem?" Hannibal stood and began pacing across his small living room.

Cindy rolled her eyes. "If that was the case you might be able to do something. No, Jason called to tell me it had all collapsed. He checked his account on line this morning and found it empty. There was nothing there. Further online investigation told him that Weston-Wellesley Investment Services had folded. There was no trail to follow, no contact information, nothing. It's just...gone. Maybe I just didn't deserve to have all that money."

She was staring at a point a thousand miles away again. How could the woman he loved be so tied up with money? There was so much more to life, yet she was acting like her life was over. He had a prepared speech for people like that who came to him for help, all about how they had their health and were loved and anybody who could build one fortune could build another and he would find the person who had stolen from them and make them pay. Looking at the pain in Cindy's eyes he couldn't bring himself to go there.

"And how did Jason find such a marvelous opportunity? Online?"

"He's not stupid," Cindy said. ""It was a personal connection, Hannibal. Someone close to the president of the company."

Probably a lie, Hannibal thought, glancing briefly at the crouching panther on his bookshelves, a figurine Cindy had bought him because she said it reminded her of him.

"That's a start," Hannibal said. He pulled his black driving gloves back on and slid his Oakley sunglasses into place. "We have a place to start. Why don't we go back to your office and talk to Jason? Maybe we can follow his connection back to the owner of the company and get some restitution."

Cindy stood, suddenly on the edge of tears. "You think it was a scam, don't you? A scheme to take money from people without much sense."

"I think it was fraud, yes. And I have some experience in this area, so why don't you let me do what I can?"

"Yes, you must have your chance to be the big hero," Cindy said, snapping to her feet. "I bet you're glad the money's all gone. It brings me back down to..." If Cindy hadn't bitten off her words and turned away, Hannibal might not have known where that sentence was going.

"To where?" He asked, a little harder than he intended. "To my level?" When she didn't respond he walked over and opened the door for her. Cindy stopped at the threshold, not looking at him but rather down at the floor. "I'm sorry lover. Really. And thank you, Hannibal, for not laughing at me."

"If you don't want anyone else laughing at you, we'd better stop by your apartment for a pair of shoes."

Approaching the outer office doors of Baylor, Truman and Ray, Hannibal considered how precious a name on the door could be to a lawyer. He knew that before the year was out that door might well say Baylor, Truman, Ray, Santiago and Moore. Of course, that might not be the direction their careers took if the world learned of a disastrous lack of judgment that left them penniless.

When Cindy pushed Jason Moore's private office door open, he spun from the window. The sandy thatch of hair was corralled into an expensive haircut. He was tall and gaunt in his thousand dollar suit, but paler than anyone should be. He looked to be Cindy's age, which meant that he left law school perhaps six or seven years before, just about when Cindy did. Moore jumped to his feet and gave Cindy what passed for a hug in the Washington business world, complete with an air kiss past her ear. Then he thrust out a hand, leaning forward over his desk.

"Hannibal Jones. Haven't seen you since my rather embarrassing performance last year at Cindy's party. We're all way too busy, man, but it's great to see you again anyway."

"I wish we were meeting up again under better circumstances," Hannibal said. "You know why I'm here?"

Hannibal looked around while Jason got up and closed the office door. His office was identical to Cindy's, big enough and tastefully decorated in a modern style. His desk was covered with papers, books, and small sheets covered with scribbled notes. A vase of lilies on a side table gave the room a slightly effeminate feel. Cindy settled into a deep visitor's chair while Hannibal dropped onto the edge of the other. Jason returned to his own seat, already squirming in it when he finally answered Hannibal's question.

"You're here about the financial difficulty I got our Cindy in, aren't you?" Jason asked. "I can't tell you how sorry I am. I called her as soon as I found out..."

"How much did you lose?"

Jason's eyes cut to Cindy. She nodded. Why were people who dealt with other people's finances every day so shy about their own, Hannibal wondered.

"I'm down about 750,000 dollars. Every cent I've managed to save since I left law school. Nothing like Cindy's loss of course, but..."

"How did you find out about this investment company that no longer seems to exist?"

Jason sat back in his chair, his eyes going to Cindy again, then back to Hannibal. "My, we are direct, aren't we?"

"We are in a hurry," Hannibal said, lacing his fingers in front of him. "We are trying to pick up the trail of a probable experienced and professional swindler before every trace of evidence evaporates and you and Cindy become just another pair of over-optimistic investors on some FBI victim's list. How'd you find out about it? Cindy thinks you know somebody."

Jason clenched his whole face, and then forced his mouth open. "I was told that investors were only invited into this opportunity by word of mouth, and that I'd better keep mum about it for fear that a stampede of investors would dilute the return. I was allowed to share the idea with one trusted person. I chose Cindy."

Hannibal's voice was dry. "How lucky for her. You know this person who shared such a wonderful opportunity?"

"Yes." Jason closed his eyes, but his fists were opening and curling in rhythm. "Irene is my...we're dating."

That brought Cindy to her feet. "Your girlfriend? Seriously? The expert adviser you told me about to convince me to hand over every cent I had in the world is your girlfriend? And you didn't tell me?"

Cindy started forward and Jason recoiled with fear in his eyes, but Hannibal grabbed the girl's arm and pulled her back to her chair. When she plopped down on the seat he turned and pointed a gloved finger at her face.

"Be still. This all just got a good deal simpler than I expected it to be. We might be able to trace her source right back to the con artist who took you." Then he turned to Jason. "Have you spoken to this Irene since you found out your investment has evaporated?" Jason shook his head. "Then get her on the phone."

"I can't."

Cindy glared. Hannibal focused on the scent of the lilies to stay calm. "You do know your lover's phone number, don't you?"

"I can't just call in the middle of the day," Jason said. "She's watched." When Hannibal raised an eyebrow, Jason added, "Her husband."

"She's married?" Cindy almost shrieked, her Cuban accent getting stronger with her anger. "You take investment advice from a bitch who's cheating on her husband?"

"We needed the money," Jason said, standing and staring into Cindy's anger. "I had to raise enough so we could take off for Mexico."

Cindy took a menacing step closer. "Not just doing another man's wife," she said, accenting every word with her hands, "but breaking up their marriage. I thought I knew you, Jason." Then she turned to Hannibal. "Honest to God, honey, he told me he got this tip from a trusted friend but never hinted even for a second that he was involved with this mystery source."

"Just give me the number," Hannibal said, turning a palm to Cindy. "I'll make the call. And put that thing on speaker."

Hannibal sat on the desk and punched in the numbers. After four rings a woman answered.

"Jason? What's wrong? You know we can't talk during the day." From the voice, Hannibal was prepared to believe that Jason was dating Dixie Carter or Paula Dean. This woman would be older than Jason, although she was still preserving her Southern belle accent.

"Ma'am, this is Hannibal Jones. I'm a private investigator and as you can see I'm calling from Jason Moore's office."

"Is he there? Is Jason all right?"

Hannibal held up a finger to stop Jason from answering. "Yes, ma'am, Jason is right here, but he's had a bad shock and we thought you might be able to help."

"It's about the money, isn't it?" Irene asked. "Oh Jason, if you're there, I'm so sorry, hon. Mine is all gone too. But I know what happened and I know who's to blame and I swear we going to make him pay."

Hannibal saw Cindy's face light up, but he knew it was too soon for celebrating. "You know who's responsible?" Hannibal asked the phone. "If that's true I might be able to help."

"I can't," Irene said. Then in a whisper she added, "Not over the phone. He might be listening, or recording or something."

"Then meet with me and if you've taken a loss I promise to help you get your money back."

"Can you help me get my life back?"

What did that mean? "I'll try. Where are you?" And why, he wondered, was she so paranoid?

"Great Falls," she replied, still whispering. "I'll look for Jason at eleven o'clock in front of the Safeway."

The line went dead.

-3-

Silence gripped the room. Hannibal was considering the conversation, trying to mentally milk all the meaning out of Irene's words and her tone.

"I don't think there's much chance it's a trap," Hannibal said. "She sounds spooked and angry. This might turn out to be easier than I expected."

"What time do you want to head up there?" Jason asked. "It's a good half hour drive. And do we meet someplace or ride in the same car?"

"We?" Hannibal said with a small smile. "No, Jason, that's not how this works. You don't go along. If you're dating this woman she'll think she can hold back with you there. And there may be things she doesn't want to admit in your presence. In fact, you don't even talk to her on the phone between now and when I see her, understand?" Jason sat back in his chair, looking unsure.

"Hannibal's right," Cindy said with a condescending tone. "Don't worry, I'll protect your interests."

"Sorry, babe," Hannibal said. "Best if I do this alone."

"No," Cindy said, stepping closer to Hannibal. "I have too much invested here. I'll go with you."

"No, you won't."

"Damn it, Hannibal, you can't just push me out of this."

Cindy was very close, in his face. Hannibal bit back his reflexive response and slid off his Oakley sunglasses. His face was passive.

"This is a mistake," he said. "I know you want to join me, but it's a bad plan."

"Well it's our plan," Cindy said.

Hannibal glanced toward Jason who was watching them very closely. Then he took Cindy's arm in a gentle but firm grip.

"Can I talk to you in your office for a minute? Please?"

After a couple of deep breaths Cindy marched out of Jason's office with Hannibal close behind. She walked to her own office and spun toward him when she was in front of her desk. Hannibal quietly closed the office door.

"Where do you get off...?" Cindy began.

"Shut up!" Hannibal's voice was sharp and low, the voice he used when he was challenged in a bar. "This is my business and you will not tell me how to do my job."

"Well if this is business then I'm the client," Cindy said, hands on hips. "I'm the one..."

"What? The one paying me? Like I'm the hired help now?" Hannibal said through clenched teeth. "You better dig yourself. What you are is the woman who invested all her money without one word to her man. Not one word, when you got an expert standing in front of you every day."

"Oh? I'm supposed to consult you about my business now?" Cindy's Cuban accent came out stronger as her voice rose. Cindy spat out her next sentence in coarse Spanish, waving her hands in Hannibal's face.

"Speak English," he said, louder than he intended.

"I said I see you every day in your dumpy little flat in Southeast. Since when are you an expert in financial matters?"

It was Hannibal's turn to get in her face. He leaned in on her, fists clenched and shaking at his sides. "No, I ain't rich, and probably never will be. What I am is an expert in fraud, schemes, and deals that are too good to be true. Not that you need to be an expert to know you don't put all your eggs in one basket. But that really don't matter right now. Right now you're in trouble. Here's the facts that matter. You're the person who got you in this fix. I'm the guy who can get you out of it. So right now you need to sit your ass down and shut the fuck up."

While he talked Hannibal poked a gloved finger at the spot between Cindy's eyes. She slowly stepped backward until she was behind her desk. Then the energy seemed to leak out of her like steam, and she lowered into her chair. Through it all she never lost eye contact with him. When she spoke again her voice was childlike and weak.

"I need to do something."

"What you need to do is go home and get some rest," Hannibal said. "What you need to do is trust me. This is what I do, after all. I'll drive up to Great Falls and get a feel for the area and scope out the meeting place in daylight. Then we'll do the meet and we'll see if I can get a trail to follow. I'll let you know what I find out first thing in the morning. Now grab your bag and whatever you absolutely need to work on today. I'm taking you home."

After dropping Cindy off, Hannibal doubled back to his own place in the District. There he did a little basic research about Great Falls and Googled up the location of the town's only Safeway. Then he moved to the kitchen and threw a steak under the broiler. While it browned he cleaned and function checked his .40 caliber Sig Sauer P229 because, well, you never know. He turned the steak, tossed a salad together, and ate in the living room watching NFL Countdown on ESPN. He didn't really care much about the team standings, but he loved the "C'mon Man" segments.

Four or five times he reached for the telephone to check up on Cindy, but each time decided not to. Twice he stood up to go talk to her father Ray, who lived upstairs from him. Both times he decided that she might not have told him what had happened, and might not want him to know. Even if she did, she would want to tell him herself.

Around seven o'clock he climbed into the Volvo he secretly called Black Beauty, cranked an obscure Jimi Hendrix blues CD and pointed west across the city. He crossed into Virginia and followed the George Washington Parkway north along the Potomac until he could hop onto the Georgetown Pike, the primary road slicing through his destination.

A pleasant forty-minute drive put him in Great Falls, which was not so much a town as a sprawling area of outsized homes and expansive wooded lots parked along the Potomac River. Named for the Great Falls National Park, the little village was a loose collection of winding roads, riding trails and country clubs. The Safeway supermarket anchored a shopping center at the intersection of Georgetown Pike and Walker Road. Across Walker sat a little village center with restaurants and shopping but, as Hannibal quickly confirmed, not one decent place to get coffee. Luckily he didn't have to go far down Route 7, back toward Tysons Corner, before he found a Starbucks. Hannibal always found them convenient places to waste a couple of hours. As long as you keep your laptop open and keep the coffee coming, nobody bothers you.

At 11 pm Hannibal left his car in the village center parking lot and walked across the two lane blacktop to the Safeway store. Everything was closed, as expected, leaving the area vacant. Traffic was nil, although a handful of cars had been left in the parking lot.

The shopping center, or strip mall as Hannibal's father would have called it, was L shaped with the Safeway store forming the short leg of the L. The space between the Safeway building and the longer building opened into a wooded area. To make things homey, someone had decided to lay a sidewalk connecting the two buildings and plant a couple of tables in the cement at the corner. Hannibal sat at one of the permanently attached chairs, working at not looking threatening. He was under one of the few streetlamps set way too far apart out there, but he doubted there was a crime problem in that area. The police always take care of the wealthy citizens, and some of the richest in the county lived in the mansions surrounding him.

The cricket serenade from the surrounding woods was so loud it almost drowned out the sound of a car door opening. The moon highlighted a blonde woman stepping out of a black Lexus, one of the vehicles parked in the lot. The black cashmere shawl across her shoulders - Cindy would have called it a pashmina - was her only practical garment, protecting her from the evening cool. Her heels not only announced her steps loudly, but would be useless if she had to run more than five steps. Like Hannibal she wore black, but her silk dress caught and reflected the moonlight, making her stand out as she walked toward him.

She hesitated as she approached him, so he stood. "I'm Hannibal Jones. You would be Irene?"

"I'm so sorry," she said, stepping to within arm's length. "I didn't expect you to be...I was afraid Wash might have sent you. He's having me followed, I'm sure of it."

Up close Hannibal saw that she was quite striking, a statuesque blonde, trim but solid, with the kind of complexion that didn't need much makeup to highlight her finely drawn features.

"UVA? By way of Alabama I'm guessing."

"How in the world?" She shook her head in feigned disbelief. "Well yes I did my time in Charlottesville, and I was born and raised in Mobile. Now where's Jason?"

Straight to the point. Hannibal liked that. "We decided it might be wiser for us to meet alone."

"Shoot. I wanted to apologize," she said. "Please tell him I am very sorry for getting him involved in all this."

"I'll pass that along. How did you two meet?"

"Well, you see, my parents passed while I was still in college," she said, waving a hand as if she was keeping rhythm with her story. "I inherited quite a little bit of money. Didn't need it, just sat there collecting interest for a while. Then I met Wash."

"Wash?" Hannibal asked as she started walking slowly along the front of the shopping center. This was a diversion, he knew. Some people had to tell a story their own way, and she would have to build toward the uncomfortable part of her tale. He presumed that was the part about committing adultery with a young lawyer. It was often more work to get people to stay on task than to let them wander toward the answers he wanted. He walked with her.

"Wash. My husband," Irene explained. "George Washington Monroe. His parents must have loved the presidents. He was a hot property at the time, an investment genius I heard. Anyway, Wash just swept me off my feet. I swear I was on my way to old maid city when he found me, last in my sorority to tie the knot. That was seven years ago."

"But things have changed?" Hannibal asked. They were approaching the tavern at the far end of the shopping center, but from the sound of things even it was empty on a week night.

"Don't get me wrong, Mr. Jones, George is a good husband and all, but he treats me like an idiot. Never lets me know a thing about his business, the finances, nothing. Gave me a fine home and a nice car and an allowance, but that's it. I am an educated woman, Mr. Jones. Anyway, I met Jason at a fund-raiser and we were like," she clapped her hands together, "POW, lightning striking, you know?"

They had reached the end of the building. Hannibal looked up and down the empty Georgetown Pike, then turned and followed her back the way they had come.

"So you wanted to help him," Hannibal said, prompting her to get on with it.

"Not right away. But Wash started getting mean to me. Ignoring me. Not touching me, if you know what I mean. And then I found out that he had a woman on the side. Probably more than one. That was enough for me. He didn't even have the decency to be embarrassed about it when I confronted him. That's when I got the idea to make Jason rich."

Hannibal nodded as they walked back through the darkness. "I see. You planned to have revenge on your husband by helping Jason cash in on an opportunity your husband was working on."

"He was very particular who he would take into his investments," she said with a sly grin. "But I managed to convince him that I knew a good prospect for him. I figured Jason would make a fortune, then I could marry him and he could support me in the style I'm accustomed to."

"But Mrs. Monroe, you have money of your own, don't you?"

"That's another thing." She stopped at the corner by the tables, under the streetlamp. "I thought about leaving Wash, but when I went to check on what was left of my trust fund I found out that Wash had emptied it out on me. I got an accountant to look into it, but he says there's no paper trail and it would be almost impossible to prove he squandered the money away. Now I got nothing of my own." Then, as an afterthought, she said, "Besides, I love Jason. I want to be with him all the time. And he loves me." Then she looked over her shoulder and moved closer to the building, partially into the shadows. "I can't stay long, Mr. Jones. I'll be missed."

"You know, Jason lost all his savings in this investment plan your husband is running," Hannibal said. "He deserves your help. And it's pretty obvious that your husband's investment plan isn't completely on the up and up."

"Honey, I don't know anything about his investments and stuff," Irene said. She was fidgeting, and Hannibal knew he was running out of time before her fear sent her home.

"I understand. Who knows him best? Do you have any friends I could trust to give me the truth?" When she clenched her lips together he added, "My woman lost all her savings too. She and Jason are friends and he thought he was doing her a favor."

"I'm so sorry," Irene said. "But getting at Wash's friends through me? That would be like going around your elbow to get to your asshole. None of them trusts me or even likes me. Except. Maybe Vera and Kevin."

Hannibal managed to stifle a chuckle when the Alabama idiom sneaked through. "Vera and Kevin? Who are they?"

"Kevin was Wash's personal assistant for a while," Irene said, getting excited and talking with her hands. "He was in the Navy, I think. Decorated war hero. Vera did cleaning around the house when Kevin worked for Wash and we got to be friends. Then Wash fired them both."

That raised one of Hannibal's eyebrows. "Were they let go because of something one of them found out?"

"I don't know. It was right after these fellows came to the house and were questioning Kevin about Wash. I thought Wash sent them in to see who knew what, so maybe. Look I've got to go."

"Just one more question, please," Hannibal said, touching her arm very lightly. "When you found out your husband had raided your trust fund, why didn't you go to the police?"

"Honey, you don't get it," she said, staring into Hannibal's eyes. "Wash is a very influential man around here. The police would all be on his side. I hired a private detective to look into it, but Wash got him run out of town. I hired an accountant to investigate but Wash scared him away."

"Well if that's true, there are people who might know something valuable," Hannibal said. Over Irene's shoulder he saw a black sedan turn off Walker Road and roll toward them, along the front of the supermarket.

The car turned left at the corner. As it passed in front of them Hannibal saw that the passenger window was half way down. Irene spun to face the car. A black tube rested on the edge of the lowered window. The tube spit fire three times with a sound like a woman's polite cough. Irene took a halting step backward. Then her head snapped back and she started to fall.

-4-

Before Irene's body hit the sidewalk Hannibal was diving forward, his pistol already drawn. He hit the ground hard, scraping his elbow on the cement. He was prepared to return fire but the engine of the black sedan roared and it sped off across the parking lot.

Hannibal hesitated for no more than a second before reaching to Irene's neck to check for a pulse. Two angry red entry wounds showed on her chest and a third glared at him from her forehead. She had been dead before her head cracked on the sidewalk.

Four seconds after the third bullet hit Irene, Hannibal was up and running along the front of the shopping center, racing toward the killer's car. The sedan was edging onto the exit to Georgetown Pike. Hannibal was panting so hard it almost drowned out the sound of his frantic footsteps. This arrogant bastard had killed the woman right in front of him. As if he was no threat. As if he was just another bystander.

"Oh, hell no," Hannibal said as the car turned right onto the street. He burst onto the road behind the car, still running hard, straining to read the license plate in the dark. As the sedan began to pull away on the open straightaway Hannibal raised his gun and fired on the run. The automatic's slide slammed back and forward, rocking the pistol in his hand five times.

Then there was nothing more he could do. He knew he had hit the car, but not the driver. The car sped away becoming smaller in the distance until it got over the first hill and disappeared. Hannibal stood for a moment with his hands on his knees and watched his murderous quarry disappear. Then he looked around. It seemed that no one had reacted to the gunfire.

Well, the houses on either side of the deserted road were all set a good hundred yards back, their privacy protected by tall trees.

Looking backward he saw that he had sprinted nearly a quarter mile trying to catch the sedan. Cursing under his breath, Hannibal began a slow walk back to the site of the killing. After a few steps he pulled out his cell phone. He considered calling Cindy, but first things first. He pushed a button to dial one of the numbers he had programmed into the phone.

"Fairfax County Police Department."

"Hello. This is Hannibal Jones, I'm a private investigator and I need to report a murder."

The Fairfax County Police Department provided law enforcement services to the citizens of Fairfax County, most of whom lived in towns too small to support a force of their own. The woman on the phone was very polite and businesslike. She walked down the list of questions although he was sure she dispatched a patrol vehicle as soon as he gave his location.

Hannibal broke into a slow jog as soon as he hung up. Sweat was sticking him to his clothes and his feet hurt from running in dress shoes, but he felt as though he deserved some discomfort right then. He had discounted Irene's fear as paranoia and now she was dead. The insult to his pride at having someone murdered right in front of him was fading and he felt ashamed of that reaction. He had lost his best lead to recovering Cindy's money. More importantly, a woman was dead. A woman whose only crime had been trying to help him.

Hannibal's steps were heavy as he headed back into the shopping center lot. The bar on the end was closed and probably was when he ran past the first time. No corroborating witness there. He trudged wearily back toward the far end of the strip mall, his head hanging. That was why he was almost back to the table and chairs when he realized that Irene was gone.

Was this someone's idea of a sick prank? The body was gone, literally without a trace. There was no blood stain on the cement. He knelt beside the place where he had pressed his gloved fingers against Irene's throat. In the dim light he would never see a stray hair or any other physical evidence but he would surely see blood.

Could she be involved in espionage, he wondered. Spy teams sometimes traveled with cleanup crews. No, that was a stretch. Going all around your elbow, he thought to himself. Occam's razor would lead him to go with the simplest theory until he proved it wrong. Any reasonably smart shooter could have had friends nearby to rush in and clean up his mess while Hannibal was gone. How long did it take him to get back to the shopping center? Five minutes? For all he knew, the shooter could have driven back around to the crime scene, cleaned up his mess and taken off again.

The police car that pulled into the shopping center was not sounding its siren or spinning its roof lights. But its headlights wrapped around Hannibal, pinning him in place until the car stopped. Only then did Hannibal notice that the police car was parked right next to the spot Irene's car should have been in.

The two uniformed white officers who got out of the car could have been brothers, or, Hannibal thought, members of the same chorus line. They were his height, six feet tall, medium build, with stringy blond hair peeking out from under their hats. One name tag said Dickens, the other Edwards. They probably stood side by side in muster formations. Both men approached with their hands on their holstered weapons. Hannibal stood slowly, keeping his hands waist high and in plain sight.

"You the guy called in the homicide?" Officer Dickens asked.

"Yes, officer. May I give you my card?" Dickens nodded. Hannibal pulled his jacket open enough to reach the lower inside pocket where he kept his cards, but not enough for the cops to see his shoulder holster. He handed the card to Dickens who read it, then handed it to his partner.

"A private detective, eh?" Edwards said. "What brings you out here? And where did the alleged homicide take place?"

"I came here to meet a client," Hannibal said. "And this is the murder scene." He pointed to the spot on the cement where

Irene's head had landed. Dickens squatted down to examine the spot, then looked up at Hannibal.

"I was talking to her when she was killed. I gave chase but the shooter got away from me. When I got back she was gone. And believe me, I know how this all sounds."

"Do you?" Dickens asked. "There would be blood. And no one reported a shooting."

"You said you came here to meet her," Edwards said. So she didn't arrive with you. How did she get here?"

Hannibal shook his head, looking down at the ground. "She drove, but her car's gone too."

Edwards pulled out a note pad and began scribbling notes. "Your client's name?"

"Mrs. Irene Monroe." The policemen looked at each other. Hannibal felt the cool evening air slipping in through his clothes. It was way too quiet for the night of a murder. Dickens cleared his throat, as if being professional and keeping a straight face was proving a challenge for him.

"Well, thank you for your help, Mr. Jones," he said. "We'll file a full report but, considering the hour, I think we'll speak with Mr. Monroe in the morning."

"In the morning? People will be tramping all over this place as soon as the stores open. Look, does either of you know Orson Rissik?"

"Is he patrol?" Edwards asked.

Hannibal blew out a frustrated puff of air. "He's a detective in your Major Crimes unit."

Both uniforms shook their heads. Dickens said, "We can find him in the morning if you think it will help. In the meantime, Mr. Jones, I'd appreciate it if you didn't leave town. We'll want to get more details from you tomorrow."

"Fine," Hannibal said. "So, is there a hotel in this town?"

Again the policemen looked at each other. Then Edwards said, "Well, there's the Hyatt Regency in Reston. It's maybe four or five miles from here."

"Fine," Hannibal said. "The computer in the car will find it for me. You guys get on back to whatever important stuff you were doing before I ruined your night."

The patrolmen didn't rise to Hannibal's sarcasm, which for some reason he found even more frustrating. They climbed back into their patrol car and drove away, leaving Hannibal alone with the questions. Who knew Irene Monroe was planning to meet him there that night? If the shooter doubled back to grab Irene's body, who took her car? And why did he or she leave Hannibal alive?

## -5-

The hotel's restaurant was called the Market Street Bar and Grill. Tastefully decorated with hardwood floors and crisp table linen, the restaurant made you think the hotel had sprung from it instead of the reverse.

It opened for breakfast at 6:30 and Hannibal was their first customer of the day. The service was swift and courteous, but Hannibal was almost too distracted to notice. Even while he was ordering his mind was on the previous evening's events and his decision not to call Cindy. It was late by the time he was on his way to the Hyatt Regency, but she would have wanted to know everything. Still, what could he tell her? He had lost his only lead. Her friend Jason had lost his lover. And Hannibal was at a loss for how to proceed.

The open-air kitchen allowed Hannibal to watch the man in white chef's gear labor artistically over his omelet. Two or three other diners entered and were seated as far from each other as possible. This was the custom in the U.S., Hannibal knew, so unlike the Germany he grew up in. Back home, strangers clung together in restaurants to share meals.

Breakfast arrived quickly, and Hannibal drank in the sharp and sweet aroma of peppers, onions, mushrooms, and a pungent cheese that may have been Monterey Jack. A good breakfast made the worst day start well.

He was chewing the very first forkful when two men entered who must have been looking for him. He knew because he recognized them from the night before. Dickens and Edwards looked as if they could both use a nap. They were still in uniform so it must have been a long night. It was okay. Aside from the fact that he wore no gloves Hannibal was also dressed exactly as he was when he met them. Of course, he had showered and changed since then, except for his suit. He guessed that his police visitors had not been so lucky.

"Mr. Jones, I'm going to have to ask you to come with us," Dickens said.

"Well, you don't have to ask me anything," Hannibal said, sipping his orange juice. "You could sit down and have some cantaloupe with me. But I imagine that your bosses have figured out what happened and have developed a sense of urgency."

"Sir," Edwards said with a slight edge to his voice, "We'll be happy to drive you to headquarters. It has been a long night and there are a couple of men in Fairfax who are eager to meet you."

Hannibal was familiar with that tone. He put his fork down with great care and stood very slowly until his nose was just a couple inches from Edwards' face. He voice was low but hard.

"Do you think I'm a felon, Officer Edwards? Are you here to arrest me? If so, let's snap on the cuffs and get moving. If not, then whoever is waiting for me can wait five more minutes while I finish this breakfast I just paid for. My night was long too. I watched a woman gunned down in front of me and I don't give a damn if you believe me or not. You want my cooperation, you sit your ass down and have a cup of coffee until I'm done."

Edwards and Dickens ushered Hannibal into an office in the Fairfax County government complex on Chain Bridge Road. The uniforms stayed outside, and only two men waited inside. It was a medium sized office just down the hall from the one he was so familiar with.

The Burly man behind the desk wore a Dick Tracy scowl and sat forward with his elbows on some scattered paperwork. His name plate said Detective Robert Carlton. Buzz cut hair and half an unlit cigar in his mouth made him a boring cliché.

The other man was far more interesting. First of all, he was black, but just a shade darker than Hannibal and a little slimmer. His hair was a very short Afro, carefully styled. His tailored suit and shoes were both stylish and expensive. He stood immediately when Hannibal entered but didn't offer a hand. Instead, his sharp, piercing brown eyes raked over Hannibal, evaluating and appraising. Hannibal felt briefly like a mouse that had caught the attention of some monstrous snake. They stood in the detective's office, but the other man spoke first.

"You are Jones?"

"That's right," Hannibal said. "And you are?"

"George Washington Monroe." Still no hand offered. "Where's my wife?"

A lot became clearer to Hannibal in that moment, and little comments and reactions from Irene and the police became clear. And Monroe's voice made it clear that he was used to getting answers when he asked questions.

"Mr. Monroe, I am very sorry. If there was anything I could have done..."

"What did you do with the car, boy?" Carlton asked.

Hannibal spun on the detective, resting a hand on the standard cheap county desk. "You mean you haven't found her car yet? Have you looked for it? And what about the crime scene? There has to be something there."

"Give it up, bud," Carlton said. "You think we're stupid? You gave the boys a good show, but the games up."

"What the hell are you talking about?"

"I've got to admit, your presence shows unexpected wit for my wife," Monroe said. He moved in front of the window so his pinstriped form was backlit, making his face hard to see. "If we were chasing around after murderers and a corpse she would have a lot more time to disappear. Unfortunately, I am not so gullible. I have already verified that they bought tickets to Canada at the train station in Alexandria late yesterday afternoon."

Hannibal looked away while his mind reconfigured the data. These men didn't think he was crazy. They thought he was part of some conspiracy to help Irene Monroe escape the area. And like most people, they probably thought all private detectives were for hire for any questionable game. Assuming that Monroe was not responsible for his wife's murder, he would have no reason to believe she was dead.

"They?" Hannibal asked, looking up. "You said they bought tickets."

"Yes," Monroe said, stepping toward Hannibal, as menacing as a man his size could be. "She and that asshole boyfriend of hers. The young lawyer, Jason Moore. How could she think I wouldn't know? But by the time I found out they were on the train it was arriving in Ontario. They could be out of the country, or they could have gotten off at any stop along the way. New York is only six hours away. Now, where are they?"

By the time he reached the end of his tirade, Monroe was directly in front of Hannibal, his fists raised as if he was about to grab Hannibal's lapels. Perhaps the fact that Hannibal had not taken a single step backward told Monroe that to grab him would be a bad idea. The two men faced each other like boxers in the ring before the bell goes off. Hannibal reached up to slip his glasses off and lock eyes with Monroe.

"I have no idea where your wife is, sport. And I have no time or patience for any man who calls me a liar."

"Hey, back off a bit there, Wash," Carlton said. So, they were on a first-name basis. Not good, Hannibal thought. Monroe took a small step backward. Hannibal smelled expensive cologne and wondered how many men would take the trouble to wear it if they were on their way to the police station because of a missing wife.

"So you're convinced she got on a train in Alexandria," Hannibal said. "So, because of that, no one has even tried to find her body. The trick you suspect worked, asshole, only in reverse."

"Watch your mouth," Carlton said. Hannibal ignored him.

"Buying a ticket doesn't mean boarding a train, you know."

"No, Monroe said, "but an eye witness does. Plus, the police found Moore's little hybrid piece of shit in the train station parking lot. Now again, where is Irene and where have you hidden her Lexis?"

Ice formed in Hannibal's stomach and he turned to Carlton. "You found Jason's car? This is not good, chief. You've got to get back to that crime scene. Turn your forensics team loose. The slug might even be there, in that little wooded space between the buildings."

"I told you, you need to give it up," Carlton said, leaning back in his chair and raising his hands behind his head. "Now why don't you tell us where they were headed before I decide to hold you for obstruction?"

Hannibal's hands trembled with frustration as he pushed his glasses back into place. "Obstruction of what? If my story's a lie, then you've got no reason to believe a crime was even committed, so what am I obstructing? Maybe you could claim I was interfering with your investigation if there was one, but I'm damned if I can see any investigation going on. And since I'm the only one who saw the lady's head hit the sidewalk, maybe I better start one."

Hannibal burst out the door and rushed past the two patrolmen in the hall. The fact that no one followed him to his car confirmed his appraisal of the situation. He wasn't regarded as a witness because no one recognized the crime he had witnessed. He beeped his black Volvo S60 open, dropped inside, started the engine and hit the button for the car phone. He needed to talk to a cop who would take him seriously.

"Orson Rissik," he said. The autodial began beeping the necessary ten tones while he pointed his vehicle east toward The District. He needed to see his woman, but even more pressing was his need to see Jason Moore.

## -6-

The law offices of Baylor, Truman and Ray were their usual beehive of commotion when Hannibal arrived. He was so familiar a sight there that secretaries and assistants all but ignored him but on this occasion a sharp call from the office manager stopped him on his way to Cindy's office.

"Mr. Jones." Mrs. Abrogast's voice cut through the buzz of activity. Mrs. Abrogast was the five-foot-two, blue-haired dynamo that kept the worker bees on task and in line, and she was the only person Hannibal knew whose stone visage could hold an arrogant smirk and an impatient scowl at the same time. Hannibal reported to her desk, as he had in the past, to accept a scolding.

"Ms. Santiago is upset about something," Mrs. Abrogast said. "She's off her game and not leading the junior associates the way she usually does. Death in the family? Illness? What?"

Hannibal smiled and dared to rest a gloved palm on her shoulder. "Yes, I'm worried about her too, but it's none of those things. She's having some personal issues."

"Well, fix it," Mrs. Abrogast said, staring into his eyes.

"Yes, ma'am," he said. "Is Jason Moore in the office?"

"He hasn't been in today. And he left earlier than usual yesterday. Does he have something to do with Ms. Santiago's issues?"

Hannibal nodded. "Is he at home?"

"It's not my day to watch him," she said, her voice dripping with sarcasm. But at the same time her right hand poked three buttons on her telephone, which was nearly as big as a computer keyboard. She never took her eyes off Hannibal's face. He heard the tones of dialing, three rings, and then Jason's voice explaining that he was out and inviting the caller to leave a message. She disconnected the line.

"I need to see Cindy right away," Hannibal said.

Mrs. Abrogast waved him on. "And when you find young Mr. Moore, you send him to me."

Hannibal moved down the hall to Cindy's office, tapped the door twice and entered. She looked up from a legal pad she was writing on behind her desk. He closed the door behind himself and stood just in front of it. He could never before remember seeing his Cindy in her office with a stray lock of hair hanging in front of her face. At home it was cute but here it was somehow chilling.

"You didn't call," she said.

"I got in late last night, and this morning I've been with the police. Where's Jason?"

Her chair squeaked as she slowly stood. "The police? What's going on? Jason didn't come in today, and he's not answering his phone. Mr. Baylor will be furious."

"Baby, I'm not sure what's going on yet." Hannibal crossed to Cindy, took her hands and eased her back down into her chair. "But I know we need to try to find Jason. The police have evidence that he ran off with Irene. Do you know any of his friends or family?"

"He doesn't talk about his family. All his friends work here, and nobody has seen or heard from him today." She looked up into his eyes, squeezing his hands. "Do you think he ran off with this woman? I can't believe he'd do such a thing."

"He may have run, but I know he hasn't run off with Irene Monroe. She's dead."

"Dead? But she was our only lead to our money." The instant the words left her mouth Cindy gasped at her own insensitivity. She tore her eyes away from Hannibal's, looking around the room for a moment. "I'm sorry. That's terrible. Poor woman. But, if the police think they ran away, well, are you absolutely sure she's dead?"

It was Hannibal's turn to shield his eyes. "I know she's dead because a drive-by shooter put three holes in her while I stood there and watched. And while I chased the shooter, somebody came along and cleaned up the body. Whoever it is set things up to make it look like your friend and his girl hopped a train out of town."

"There's no way Jason would run out, especially if someone he loved was in trouble," Cindy said. "But... oh, God. If someone killed her, then..."

"Let's not jump to any conclusions," Hannibal said. "He could just as likely be hiding from whoever took out Irene. We need to find the truth. I know you called Jason's house but has anybody been over there today?" When Cindy shook her head, he said, "Then that's my first stop."

Hannibal bent to give Cindy a light kiss, but as he headed for the door he heard her footsteps behind him. He turned to ask what else she needed, but she cut him off.

"I'm coming with," she said.

"Bad idea, babe," "Oh, Hannibal, I can't just sit here not knowing. Please."

Jason's townhouse was in the Northwest part of the District in Brentwood, not far off New York Avenue. In theory, it's easy to get out of the city from there, but Hannibal imagined Jason's morning commute into the heart of DC must have been ugly. The house was tall and narrow, as if its neighbors were squeezing it in. The tiny splash of front yard was less than Hannibal had in front of his place, a relative tenement, but Jason's was lush and green, carefully tended and filled with exotic plants Hannibal couldn't name. They created a small bubble of sweet fragrance around the front door. Hannibal went up the stairs to it with Cindy close behind. He rang the bell, waited ten seconds and then knocked. Then he tried the door.

"If he's here, he's a heavy sleeper."

"He could be lying in a pool of blood in there," Cindy said. "Call the police?"

"What?" she grunted in frustration. "Can't you pick the lock or something?"

"That's breaking and entering, and you are an officer of the court."

Cindy hesitated maybe two seconds. "I am a personal friend and he invited me in. I have a reasonable suspicion that this is an emergency. I thought I heard a scream from inside, and the prudent man…"

"Okay, okay." Hannibal raised a palm in surrender. "One good excuse will do. Give me a second."

"So you can pick the lock?" Cindy moved closer to shield him from view while staring over his shoulder.

"No need. I have a key." One of the keys on the ring Hannibal pulled out of his pocket was a bump key, the kind developed in Denmark several years ago. It was actually a modified key blank designed to defeat typical pin tumbler locks. He slid it into the lock one notch out. Then he pulled out his pocket knife, a one-handed folder that clipped onto his pants pocket. He then used the end of the knife to bump the key inward. The specially designed teeth of the key jiggled all the key pins in the lock. The key pins transmitted the force to the driver pins, which separated from the key pins for a split second and were pushed back by the spring, allowing Hannibal to turn the key and open the door.

"Teach me to how to do that?" Cindy asked as they stepped inside.

"Not on your life."

Hannibal and Cindy took a quick walk-through, just to establish that no one was lying dead on any of the floors. Jason's townhouse was neat for a bachelor's home, with the kind of carpet and furniture Hannibal associated with mobile homes. It appeared to be a real estate investment rather than a sanctuary, furnished with either the first or the cheapest furniture Jason found.

"What now?" Cindy asked when they returned to the front room on street level.

"Now we look for some clue as to where your friend Jason took off to."

"He wouldn't just take off," Cindy said. Hannibal held his reply, exploring the coat closet instead. Nothing shouted unexpected trip to him, but without knowing how many coats or how much luggage the man had, how would he know?

The living room looked sterile. A few hotel-style pictures hung on the walls, but no flowers or knickknacks personalized the space. Apparently the living room was simply a space Jason walked past on his way to the useful part of the house.

The kitchen and den showed some signs of use. There were dishes in the dishwasher but none in the sink. The refrigerator and cupboards held basic foods in normal amounts.

"Is he always this neat?" Hannibal asked.

"Jason? He's a total neat freak. Except when it comes to work. Hannibal, why are you doing this?"

"What do you mean?"

"You know what I mean. I'm not a client and the police would handle a missing persons case, right?"

"Babe, I'm here right now because somebody swindled my woman out of a lot of money and Jason is our only trail to getting it back." He lifted the garbage can lid. The bag was gone. Well, a neat freak would set the trash outside if he planned to be gone a few days.

"I know I'm not wrong about the money thing," Cindy said while Hannibal looked around what would be the family room if Jason had a family. "It kind of came between us and that was my fault I know. But still, I think you'd just as soon I never got it back. Or am I wrong?"

The entertainment center held a flat screen television and five of its six shelves held figurines apparently purchased just to keep them from being vacant. That made Jason's life look empty. The top right shelf held the only framed photo. Jason stood at the right edge of a smiling five person group, all the same age, all well-dressed. Cindy stood beside him.

"Is this right after graduation?"

"The next day, as a matter of fact," Cindy said. "Are you being evasive?"

"I'm trying to be focused," Hannibal said. "Someone you care about has gone missing. You care about him. That makes him important to me. Don't you want to know what happened to your friend?"

Three bedrooms shared the second level. One was an antiseptic guest room. Jason used the other as office. Hannibal sat at the desk, facing the computer with a futon behind him that could be folded down into a bed. A pair of prescription glasses lay in front of the keyboard. Stacks of paper stood on either side of the computer, and a chaos of paper covered the futon behind him like a deck of oversized cards that had been fanned out in preparation for a magic trick. This was the kind of disorder a man created while working, not the random mess that would result from someone searching through the documents.

"Of course I want to know where he is," Cindy said, trailing Hannibal to the master bedroom. "But I know you usually try to avoid work the police would do. Especially if there's no pay involved."

"They won't look for Irene Monroe," He said while exploring Jason's dresser. One pair of cuff links were missing, several other sets remained. No robbery, then.

"Well, she's not a client either."

She followed him into the walk-in closet. There was a place for everything, leaving obvious holes for missing items. Hannibal closed his eyes, resisting the urge to fill the silence, but ultimately losing.

"Damn it, Cindy, the woman was killed right in front of me. She trusted me, and now she's dead. I can't just let that lie. And your boy may be running from whoever did it. Look here. There's a couple of suits missing here, two pair of shoes and looks like three ties. Looks like Jason was packing for a short trip."

"I can't believe that," Cindy said as they moved to the bathroom. "He'd never take off, not without telling Mr. Baylor. Not without telling me."

"Well so far it looks like Jason does quite a bit without telling you," Hannibal said, poking through drawers and the medicine cabinet. "I'm not seeing a toothbrush. No comb. No cologne or deodorant. When the police stop by they'll think the same thing. He packed quick and hit the road."

"That doesn't prove anything."

"Cindy, maybe you don't get it, but if Jason is in hiding that's good news." Then he stopped talking. He slowly lifted a small plastic container out of a drawer. The little figure-eight-shaped tray was the kind people put contact lenses in to soak. He blinked at himself in the wall length mirror over the double sinks and his mouth set in a grim line.

"Did Jason wear glasses?"

"Well, contacts," Cindy said.

"No, I mean regular glasses with frames."

"Never," Cindy said. "The only time I saw him in real glasses was that time last year when he lost one of his contacts. I told him he should have two pair but his prescription is weird I guess so the lenses are expensive so he only had one pair. Why? Is that important?"

Hannibal opened the little container. Two lenses floated there in a few drops of solution. "Shit," he muttered under his breath.

"What?"

"Jason would have put them there at night and put them in his eyes in the morning. A regular routine every day. He'd never have left the house without them. And I saw his glasses in the office so he's not wearing them."

"See, he didn't run off," Cindy said, but the note of triumph in her voice faded quickly. "So where is he?"

Hannibal put the lenses back where he found them and headed down the stairs. "Gone. They took him last night."

## -7-

"They?" Cindy asked. "What they?"

"Whoever hit Irene Monroe," Hannibal said. He walked through the sliding glass door into Jason's postage stamp back yard. A few steps later he opened the gate and stepped out into the alley behind the house. Even in the middle of the afternoon it was quiet. Trees overhung the alley from the yards on both sides. It was just wide enough for a garbage truck to pass through. Jason's large trash can stood right beside the gate. Hannibal looked up and down the alley and muttered, "It would be so easy here."

"You're scaring me," Cindy said.

"I'm sorry babe, but it only fits together one way. There was no bag in the kitchen trash can."

"I told you he was a neat freak," she said. "If he was going to be gone he'd take out the trash before he left."

"Sure, but a real neat freak would have put a new bag in the can as soon as he got back from taking the garbage out. I figure he came out here to toss the trash and they just scooped him up. Then they went inside just long enough to grab stuff to make it look like Jason left on his own. Buying more time. They really thought this out."

"But why take Jason away?"

Hannibal turned to stare into Cindy's eyes. The setting seemed altogether too idyllic for this conversation, but he had to get through to her. "I saw Irene Monroe die. Somebody wants the world to think she ran off with her boyfriend. Get it? For them to sell the idea that Irene just disappeared, Jason had to disappear too. I'm afraid he's..."

"Being held somewhere," Cindy said, forcing her words over Hannibal's. "Oh, Hannibal, he's probably tied up someplace, maybe hurt."

Hannibal turned his back to Cindy, staring down the alley to the cross street as if he could somehow see which way the abductors went. He knew there was no reason for them to keep Jason alive.

"I hate that you got tied up with this whole thing. These people are cunning and dangerous and probably desperate to keep whatever they're doing under the radar. Why didn't you come to me before investing all that money in their crazy scheme?"

After a pause, Cindy said, "I tried hard not to talk to you about money at all." When Hannibal turned to her, she almost broke down. "I'm sorry. It kind of made me feel like you thought I was being superior or something. I'd have felt like, you know, an insult to injury thing. Like, 'Hey look, I'm rich and I'm about to get richer.' Come on, Hannibal, I get it. Even I used to think rich people suck. Then they let me in their club."

Hannibal rested a hand on her arm. "Yeah, but you'd have never got that attitude, not like that crowd out in Great Falls. Irene's husband sure has it, but I don't think she ever caught it. How'd Jason ever hook up with her anyway?"

"Oh, that was at one of those meet and greet cocktail party things," she said as they went back into the house. "We do those things all the time and it's always politely professional. But when he heard that laugh of hers and that southern belle accent he just fell. Hard."

Hannibal led her back into the townhouse. No more to do here. "Did you like her?"

"Oh, I hated her at first. Seemed like she was using him just to take care of her urges while she was married to an older guy. But she made Jason happy. And then he hinted that she was talking about leaving her man for him. And then she came up with the offer to push Jason to a new financial level."

"Yeah, and taking you along with him." Hannibal held the front door for Cindy and closed it behind them. "She had the look of a trophy wife, but I'm sure there are lots of people just like you who will say they're not surprised Jason and Irene would run off together. Especially if they've met Monroe and got a feel for how he treated her."

Back in Hannibal's car, Cindy let out a long sigh. "They won't look very hard, will they?"

"Depends on how much pressure they get. Do his folks have connections?"

"Jason lost his parents in a terrible accident the year he graduated law school." Cindy shook her head, eyes clenched. "No brothers or sisters either. Jason just doesn't have any family to prod police to keep searching. Oh, Hannibal, what can we do?"

"I might have an idea, but I need to make a stop first."

Hannibal pulled his black Volvo to the curb near the street lamp directly across the street from his building. Very soon after he moved there, the neighborhood seemed to reach an unspoken agreement that this parking space belonged to him. It was an odd expression of respect in Southeast D.C., and he took it very seriously. Beside him, Cindy sat silent and motionless. He figured she was still processing all they learned at Jason's house. He leaned over and placed a gentle kiss on her cheek.

"Why don't you wait here, babe. I won't be but a minute."

Hannibal hurried across the street and up the red sandstone steps leading to the front door of his red brick, three-story building. The main door was only locked at night, so he pushed it open and stepped into the dark hallway. The pine scent told him that one of his neighbors had mopped the main hall for him. Hannibal appreciated the gesture. After all, it was Hannibal's responsibility since he rented the entire first floor.

He faced the central staircase but instead of turning right to the apartment that served as his office he moved to his left toward his residence. He walked back to the fourth door, which was his apartment's front door. For the hundredth time he told himself that eventually he would drywall over those other doors, which were remnants of the days when the five rooms of his flat were rented separately.

He unlocked his door and, once inside, keyed the pass numbers into his alarm system to shut it off. Then he sprinted to his bedroom hoping to complete his mission before anyone noticed he was in the building. As much as he liked the other men who lived in his building, he really didn't want to stop to chat with anyone.

Laying a suit bag out on the bed he grabbed a couple of almost identical black suits, white dress shirts and dark ties. A couple of casual choices, underclothes and personal care items, and he was ready for a few days away. After a quick glance out the window at his girl, still waiting in the car, he turned toward the door.

He found himself staring into Ray Santiago's concerned face.

"Hey, Hannibal, what's going on man?" Ray asked around the stub of a cigar. "You rushing out again?"

Reynaldo Santiago was short and bulky, with that dark yet light complexion that seemed exclusive to those who had immigrated from Cuba. All his remaining hair clung to sides and back of his head. The toughest little cab driver in the District, Ray had helped Hannibal chase the drug addicts out of the building, and then moved upstairs when Hannibal moved in on the first floor. He was one of Hannibal's closest friends. Usually that fact was not at all affected by his also being Cindy's father.

"Yeah, Ray, I'm on a case. Can't stop to talk."

"Uh-huh." Ray stretched out a hand to stop Hannibal's forward motion. "What's going on with my Cintia? She hasn't answered my calls."

The use of her full name told Hannibal that Ray knew something wasn't right. "I think she's going through some stuff right now Ray."

"What kind of stuff?" Ray asked, crossing his arms. "Stuff she's keeping to herself? Or stuff she tells you about but not her poppy?"

"I think maybe stuff she's not ready to tell you yet," Hannibal said, edging toward the door. "I'm sorry Ray, but I don't think it's my place to tell you her business if she hasn't."

The two men locked eyes for a few long seconds. Then Ray took a step back, allowing Hannibal to pass. As Hannibal set one foot past the threshold Ray's hand settled on his shoulder for a moment.

"You take care of my little girl, Paco."

Hannibal nodded and hustled outside. He tossed his bag into the trunk and got into the driver's seat without looking back. He didn't want to know if Ray had followed him and saw Cindy in the car.

"That was quick," Cindy said as he started the car.

"Not as quick as I hoped."

"So what now?" Cindy asked. "I still don't see how we're going to find the people who took Jason away."

"Our best hope is that Irene's killers tried too hard and left some evidence of their crimes," he said, pulling away from the curb. "They left quite the trail of breadcrumbs to lead detectives to the conclusions they wanted, but it's damned difficult to make it perfect. So we pick at the clues and try to pull them apart. We found some things that didn't look right at Jason's house. And according to Rissik, left Jason's car at the Alexandria train station. Let's go see what might not look right there."

In the life of a private detective, things are seldom as simple as they should be. Hannibal reflected on that idea while he and Cindy wandered the Alexandria Union Station, the city's historic train station. From the small parking area of the tiny way station, built just after 1900, they looked up at the Masonic Washington Monument at the Western end of Alexandria's Old Town. It took less than a minute to ascertain that Jason's silver Toyota Prius was not parked in the little lot. They explored the nearest restaurant parking lot. They even walked the streets a block in each direction before accepting that it was nowhere in the area.

Hannibal could not rule out the idea that Carlton, or even some members of the Fairfax County police, were part of the Irene Monroe conspiracy, but he didn't see any good reason for them to lie about Jason's car. He knew lots of way to try to find out what had happened but he always favored trying the easy things first. So, he let his eyes wander to the three people waiting on the benches outside the train station.

The young guy at the far end of the nearest bench was only outside to get a smoke. Probably not there for very long. The Latin man on the middle bench had rough hands and wore working clothes. He was very likely illegal. He would not see anything and would not want to answer any questions. The older black woman at the far end wore mules over nylon knee highs that ended just below the hem of her black skirt. She was travelling with a shopping bag full of stuff. She was outside because there was nothing to look at inside. He waved to Cindy to follow and walked over to her.

"Excuse me ma'am. Could you help us? We can't seem to find our car."

"Well I didn't take it."

Hannibal chuckled a little. "No, I'm sure you didn't. My friend borrowed the car to drive to the train station and said he'd leave it parked in this lot. It's not worth stealing, it's a little thing, a silver Prius."

"That little silver thing?" the woman asked. "Child, they towed it away almost an hour ago. You going to have to pay to get it back. You better get on your friend for that money."

"Towed it?" Hannibal looked shocked. "Oh no. How am I going to find it? Did you notice the name of the company?"

"Nope. But there was a police car here at the same time, and the cop was kind of directing them. Was your friend dealing drugs or something? I figured there must have been something important in the car."

Hannibal looked at Cindy in horror, thanked the woman, and rushed into the train station. Once inside his expression returned to its usual calm acceptance.

"You really got into character for that one," Cindy said.

"That was only half faked. It sounds like the county towed Jason's car. I didn't think the detective I talked to was that smart."

"I don't get it," Cindy said. "Why would they tow Jason's car away if they think he took the train to disappear."

"That's just it, babe. They wouldn't. The only reason to pull in his car is to go over it for clues. And they'd only do that if someone suspected foul play. And I think I know who that someone is."

"Then we need to go find where the car is, right?"

"No," Hannibal said. "Time is short. The cops are already working on whatever the car will give up. All that forensic stuff. We need to do what they're not doing. Cover the path they might have missed."

"Okay, like what?"

Hannibal did a slow pan across the terminal. Half a dozen benches lined up across the floor and sunlight from a skylight above gave the room the feel of a small church, despite the peeling green paint and older, stained floor tiles. Anxious children seemed mismatched with bored or frustrated adults who would be at an airport if they could afford it. The kids occasionally ran through the open spaces in random patterns, causing the adults to hold their luggage close. A human circus without a ringmaster, he thought. No ringmaster, but this human hell did have a gatekeeper.

Aloud he said, "Like checking if anyone can confirm what the cops were told last night."

A small trapezoid boxed off in a corner of the station held the modern day Cerebus in place. She was somewhere between thirty and fifty years old, wearing deep blonde in a smart, short style, lipstick that was too bright for her pale complexion and a permanently furrowed brow. No one could pass through to the train platform without first paying her their respects. She wore her official status like a cloak, as if it was power. Hannibal put on his official expression too, stepped up to the narrow window of the ticket counter and pressed his credentials against the side of her glass prison.

"Hello, Miss Stone," he said, reading the unlikely name on her metal nametag. I'm working a missing person's case and could use your help. Were you on duty last night?"

She nodded but stayed silent. So this was how it was going to go, he thought.

"Ma'am, do you remember a young couple that bought tickets for Canada last night? The man would have been very thin and pale, neatly dressed with brown hair and eyes. The woman was attractive, tall, blonde and blue-eyed, with an Alabama accent."

Stone nodded again. "I don't remember any accent, and I would have noticed," she said, displaying her own honeyed Georgia tones. "But it sounds like the same couple the police asked me about. They were the last tickets I sold yesterday, around five o'clock."

Cindy squeezed her eyes shut. She had already stopped, right where the police would, but for Hannibal the interview was incomplete.

"Did they seem nervous to you? In a hurry?"

Stone shrugged. "He was maybe."

"Do you remember anything else about them? Anything at all? Their luggage or their clothes perhaps?"

Stone leaned closer to the window, her clear hazel eyes suddenly more alert. "There's more to this, isn't there?"

Hannibal also leaned closer and lowered his voice. "What's your first name?"

"Lane," she said, dropping her grim demeanor. She did have a winning smile.

"Well, Lane, they may have met with… foul play. It could be a kidnapping. There might be a reward." Hannibal slid his card through the slot. "I'd be willing to split it if there is. Do you remember anything else?"

Stone's hand fell on the card, her fingers touching Hannibal's. Her eyes closed and rolled upward as if she was searching her mental attic. Her brow furrowed more deeply, and her mouth dropped open a couple of seconds before she began to speak.

"You know, the tat seemed out of place."

Hannibal glanced at Cindy, whose eyes popped open at Stone's comment. "A tattoo?"

"Yeah," Stone said. "I mean, here's this guy in a nice suit and tie and all, hair cut nice and neat, and there's this tat sticking up out of his collar, like a flame or something. I mean I'm looking at him and it's like, what's wrong with this picture?"

Hannibal stared at Cindy who clenched her lips together so tightly that her lower lip poked out and shook her left to right.

"You've been a big help, Miss Stone," Hannibal said.

"It's Lane," she said.

"Well, Lane, I'll be in touch about that reward if this pans out."

"Hey, just call when you know something, okay?" she said. "Usually people just blow by. Sometimes I make up stories about where they're going and what they'll do when they get there. I'd just kind of like to know what happened to them."

Hannibal promised to keep her informed, Cindy thanked her, and they headed back to the car. As soon as they were outside again Hannibal said, "I don't remember Jason having a tattoo that showed over his collar."

"I remember us talking in law school about how things like tattoos or piercings could hurt your career. Believe me, he'd never consider it. So now we talk to the police, right? We've got solid evidence that it wasn't them that got on the train yesterday. At least, it wasn't Jason."

"No, it's still too soon," Hannibal said, opening the door for Cindy and watching her perfect legs swivel up and into place in the car. He closed her door and walked around to get behind the wheel.

"So what else can we do?" Cindy asked as he started the Volvo. "I don't see how we can know who the imposters were who got on the train yesterday, and by now they could be anywhere."

"Hey, we know they were imposters," Hannibal said. "That's a valuable piece of the puzzle. And we know some valuable things about them. But we also know some other things the police don't know, things they don't care about because they're investigating a disappearance while we're investigating a murder."

Cindy leaned her head back and sighed. "Okay, Sherlock, what do we know?"

Hannibal poked at his sound system controls and the tight harmony of The Temptations filled the vehicle. Then he nudged the climate control to a slightly higher temperature. "Irene told me that she had gone to an accountant to try to prove that her husband had milked her inheritance. With some legwork I might be able to figure out who she talked to, and he might be able to add a motive to our murder theory."

"I'll bet we won't have to search," Cindy said, turning the temperature setting back down. "Here's what I think. If Irene and Jason were that tight she'd have asked him who to get, and he'd have recommended one of the CPAs we work with at the firm."

"Hey, that's a great start," Hannibal said with a smile. "How many accountant firms do you work with?"

"As I think about it, they'd want to be low profile," Cindy said, poking the button to switch the stereo to radio play. One of those rappers who uses only initials for his name burst into the car. Cindy was bobbing her head to the beat while she spoke. "That would mean Paul Queen. He's an independent, not part of a big firm, but very discreet." She began to rhyme along with the tune.

Hannibal stopped at a light, his eyes clamped shut for a second, his teeth clenched tight. Then the moment passed. His right hand moved to the console, pressing the button that returned The Temptations to the airwaves.

"Look here," Hannibal said, eyes straight ahead as he drove through the intersection. "I'll be too hot for you. I'll be too cold for you. But the driver picks the music, all right?"

While Hannibal pointed his Volvo down Route 1 out of Alexandria toward Washington DC, Cindy faced away from him to call her office. Before they had passed the Ronald Reagan National Airport she had gotten all she needed on Paul Queen from Mrs. Abrogast. By the time Hannibal was driving across the 14th Street Bridge she had made a second call to Queen's office where she was able to confirm that his schedule was open that day. When she announced her success, Hannibal gave her thigh an encouraging pat.

Queen's office was down on M Street, a couple of blocks due south of Dupont Circle. Hannibal was stunned to find a parking space within easy walking distance on Connecticut Avenue. He took it as an omen that life was getting better. He was marching toward their destination when Cindy tugged on his arm.

"Hey, we've been running all morning. Buy a girl lunch?"

Hannibal expected her to be in a hurry but now it seemed she wanted to slow the pace. It was his nature to drive forward as long as he could see the trail on a case, but Cindy seemed delicate right then. Maybe she needed time to digest what they had before they had to swallow new input about her dead friend. He looked around for a good compromise and pointed at the first option he saw.

"How about DGS, right there?"

DGS was a real delicatessen. The atmosphere was loud, the service fast, the food solid and good. Not a place for a business meeting, DGS was where you went when your only objective was to eat. It smelled delicious. And it was one of the few places in The District that reminded him of his days as a cop in New York. He stepped to the counter with Cindy peering over his shoulder.

"Hey, buddy! I need a hot pastrami on rye with mustard, and she'll have," he turned to Cindy, "a Reuben, right?"

"You know me too well."

"And to split, some... coleslaw?"

"Oh, potato salad," Cindy said, flashing a real smile. "Theirs is real good."

"Yep. That and a couple cokes will do it."

They settled into one of the tables-for-two lining the brick wall facing the counter. Food came quickly and Hannibal wasted no time biting into his sandwich. It was as juicy and flavorful as any he had ever gotten in Manhattan. He grinned at Cindy and she returned his smile as she bit into her own lunch. Then she seemed to darken and she chewed more slowly. Her foot touched his under the table. When she swallowed, he was ready.

"Hannibal. Honey. I'm sorry for that... you know, in the car."

"It ain't even a thing," Hannibal said. "Forget it." He hesitated to say, "I get it," but in fact he understood and regretted his sharp words. Of course she wanted to be in control. After all that had happened in the last twenty-four hours she wanted to feel that she was in control of something. It should have been okay for it to be him.

"You are always so sweet to me," she said, eyes down. "Too sweet." He gave her a wink and continued with his lunch. The chatter in the deli made it easier to eat without conversation. He was watching her when he bit into his slice of kosher dill pickle. He saw her eyes flash on something and then return to the table.

"What?"

"Nothing."

He reached for her hand. "No. What?"

"Well, okay, this accountant. Paul Queen." She looked into his eyes, almost daring them to lie to her. "Seriously, do you think this could be a real lead to your murderer and my swindler? Or are you just humoring me?"

He smiled and squeezed her hand. "Babe, I wouldn't waste time when we're trying to solve this thing just to humor you. In my life, this is how it works. Welcome to the world of the private detective. I follow whatever trail surfaces until it runs to a dead end, then I pick up another one. I can't be sure if this trail will lead to where we want to go, but it's what we've got right now, and yes, it is a legitimate lead. So let's go see where it might lead to."

The short walk to their destination was not enough to work off the sandwich and Hannibal knew he would need to do a little extra road work later on. Cindy kept up with his pace and again appeared eager to make some progress. They found the right building and then the right suite. Just before they walked in, Cindy stopped Hannibal to wipe a dot of mustard from the corner of his mouth. She gave him a soft kiss to that corner, took a deep breath, and turned to the door.

Inside, a very plain secretary told them that she had informed Mr. Queen about their phone call and that he would in fact be very happy to speak with them. She stood up from her very plain wooden desk to lead them the twelve paces to the inner office door. She opened it and ushered them inside with a wave of her hand. Hannibal followed Cindy inside to stand in front of a larger, yet still very plain wooden desk.

The man behind the desk looked up and smiled, and then lurched to his feet to shake their hands. He was a big man, easily three hundred pounds with a round bald head and thick fingers. With his suit jacket off his body looked gelatinous inside his white shirt, as if the shirt were holding his mass together. He wore suspenders and his sleeves were rolled halfway up his arms. The term "jolly old elf" came into Hannibal's mind.

"Please, have a seat. I understand you know Irene Monroe. Fine lady."

"I met her," Hannibal said, settling down on a ladder backed chair as Queen squished back into his own. "Have you heard from her in the last few days?"

Queen rolled forward, resting his arms on the desk. "Miss Santiago, are you part of the team looking for her? I'm afraid I don't know anything that would help you find her. And I'm not so sure I'd tell you if I did."

"You've heard she ran off," Cindy said. Queen nodded. Cindy turned to Hannibal. Queen's eyes followed.

"Mrs. Monroe has not run away," Hannibal said. "She is in fact dead. She was murdered."

Queen leaned back, and Hannibal thought he smelled bacon grease. "You're shitting me," the accountant said.

"This is very real," Hannibal said.

"That just doesn't make any sense," Queen said. "Why is the news saying she took off to Canada or someplace?"

"Because whoever wanted Irene Monroe dead is very clever," Hannibal said. "In order to make the runaway story stick they got a substitute to buy a ticket in Irene's name and get on a train headed north. I know it sounds crazy, but believe me, she was gunned down in the street. I saw it happen. I just can't prove it."

Queen nodded into his neck. "So you're not here looking for her. You're looking for the killer. Or maybe you think you know who it is and you're looking for a motive. Am I right?"

"Paul, I know there are issues of client confidentiality here," Cindy said, leaning forward. "We don't want to pry into the details of her personal business. We just want to know why she hired you."

"Hey, I ain't no lawyer," Queen said, pulling a large handkerchief out of his hip pocket. "I only protect client information to protect them. Doesn't sound to me like Irene needs any more protecting. Besides, I think you're on the right track. You're looking at the husband, right?"

"What makes you think so?" Hannibal asked.

"Irene came to me because she was worried about her money," Queen said, wiping his face with the handkerchief. "She had a little piece of a trust fund when she got married, sort of an emergency fund her daddy left her. Well, as she put it, George Washington was a speculative business man, with a lot of ups and downs. He kind of steered her away from checking on her trust fund, so she wanted me to see if it was invested well."

"Yes," Cindy said. "Mr. Washington seems to have the golden touch with money."

"Yeah? Not from what I could see," Queen said. "I got a good long look at that account and the fund itself was shrinking over time. From what I could see, he kept putting her money into losing investments. On the surface it looked like he was a pretty poor investor, consistently betting on investments that cost him money."

Queen fell silent, looking into Hannibal's lenses. Hannibal watched his face closely. "You said, 'on the surface.' What do you think was going on underneath."

Now it was Queen's turn to lean forward and lower his voice. "I think he was purposely stealing her money out from under her. There was evidence that he was making deals that were plausible on the surface, but unwise if you looked closer. I think he was unloading her assets through dummy setups. Sort of like selling stuff to himself. Then he would buy it back from himself on the cheap, through another company. It's real smooth, almost invisible, unless you happen to be a CPA who has seen this kind of thing before."

"All right!" Cindy said, sliding to the edge of her chair.

"It wouldn't be enough to open a murder investigation," Hannibal said.

"No, but if we take this to the police it should prompt them to investigate Monroe's finances. He's probably got my money too, and Jason's."

Cindy's sudden enthusiasm shook Hannibal as much as her comments did, but before he could gather the words for a response he was distracted by a chuckle that bubbled up out of Paul Queen like gas escaping the La Brea tar pits.

"Ms. Santiago, really. There is nothing to take to the police."

"But you said..."

"I said there was some evidence. My nose tells me that this guy's finances aren't on the up and up. But to prove it? To dig through the layers of shell companies and dummy corporations owned by other dummy corporations? Well, give me a half dozen good forensic accountants and get me full access to

Monroe's records and a year or so to go through them and I could give you something you could take to court."

Cindy gripped Hannibal's sleeve. "You used to work at Treasury. Can't you get them or the IRS to look into this guy's business dealings?"

"They'd need some kind of event as an excuse." Hannibal had said it out loud before he put it together. "Paul, if this guy's wife is dead, that's a real good excuse to evaluate his entire estate, right? For estate tax purposes. Maybe a missing wife is just as good an excuse."

Cindy and Queen said, "No," at the same time. Queen continued, "They won't move on her until she's declared dead. Unless they turn up her body that gives this guy seven years to reconfigure his finances or shift it all overseas, or just disappear to another country himself."

Cindy closed her eyes, shaking with frustration. "He's too smart. How can we get at this guy?" It was a rhetorical question, but Queen answered.

"Well, you could look for the one guy who might know all about his financial dealings, his old business partner."

"He had a partner?" Hannibal asked.

Queen sat back, smug in that way people are when they think they have all the answers you need. "Yep. Manny Hernandez. Monroe is like Teflon, nothing sticks to him, but Hernandez was a little shady. They don't run together no more but I'm betting Hernandez knows where all the bodies are buried." Cindy's shiver must have made Queen realize what he had said because he interrupted himself to say, "Sorry. Poor choice of words. But if Hernandez is sore about being cut out of whatever Monroe is doing he might be happy to talk about it."

"That's a good lead," Hannibal said. "Any idea where…?" The ring of his cell phone cut him off. With an exasperated sigh he pulled it out and flipped it open.

"Where the hell are you?" Detective Orson Rissik growled. "Am I going to have to solve your case all by myself?"

## -8-

Rissik had not called Hannibal to his office in the Fairfax County municipal complex, but rather asked to meet him in the county impound lot. Hannibal led Cindy down the rows of vehicles until they found Rissik, standing with his arms crossed, leaning back against Jason's Prius. In his tan suit and straw colored crew cut he looked like any average businessman except for the dangerous blue eyes and perpetually bitter expression.

"Good morning, Miss Santiago," he said, and then looked at Hannibal. "So, I hear you gave Carlton a hard way to go."

"Yeah, I suppose I did, but…"

"Good! He was being an idiot, making bad assumptions about a source I already told him is trustworthy. So Major Crimes took it over. It's my case now."

"Well that's good news. Did you check out the crime scene?"

"Of course," Rissik said. "I didn't think there'd be anything to see in a shopping center on a weekday twelve hours after the reported crime. But it turns out these crime scene boys can do pretty amazing things these days. The right chemicals brought up blood stains in the cement right where you said they'd have to be. And an hour or so rummaging around in that little wooded area between the buildings turned up a spent thirty-eight caliber slug."

"No casing?" Cindy asked. Rissik gave her the "why are you here" look. Hannibal knew she was simply repeating what she had heard on too many television shows.

"The .38 is more often a revolver round, babe. They don't throw the empty case like an automatic does. You have to dump them out when they're empty."

"None of that verifies a murder," Rissik said, crossing his arms. "I was kind of hoping you could give me a little more."

"Well, if you discount your eye witness it's all pretty circumstantial. I've got an accountant who will testify that Monroe snaked the cash out of Irene's trust fund, so maybe a motive. And the ticket girl at the Alexandria train station can verify that the couple who got on the Amtrak headed north wasn't Jason Moore and Irene Monroe. At least, it wasn't Jason."

Rissik nodded. "It sure sounds like some sort of conspiracy, but you're right, it sure ain't proof."

"No, but I've got a feeling you've got more. What did you get off the car?"

"What makes you think I got something off the car?" Rissik asked with a sarcastic smile.

"Come on, Orson. You made us trek out here to the car. So what did you find?"

"Nothing. The car's wiped clean." Then he looked up at Hannibal with a sly smile.

"What?" Cindy's distress was clear. "Nothing? No fingerprints? No hairs or fibers or whatever? Why are we out here then?"

Hannibal held up a palm to calm her. "Will you relax? Orson, am I reading you right? No prints at all?"

"That's right, some moron wiped it all down. Door handles, steering wheel, everything. They'd have been a lot better off wearing gloves."

"So not only did somebody else drive Jason's car, but that wasn't their original plan." Then to Cindy he said, "If Jason had driven to the train station, at least his prints would be on the door handles, the steering wheel, rear view mirror and so on."

"A smart snatch artist would wait until he got in the car, bum rush him then, and make him drive wherever they wanted him. It's easy to control somebody when *they* have to watch the road and *your* hands are free."

Hannibal closed his eyes to picture the scene. "But he must have spotted them before he was in the car. I checked the area and can see exactly where they could take him with no risk of prying eyes."

Cindy walked around to look into the driver's window, almost as if she could imagine her friend in the seat. "Oh, Jason, where have they taken you?"

Orson stepped closer to Hannibal and lowered his voice a bit. "You know he's dead, right? Even if this is all about the girl, they'd have no reason to keep this guy alive so he could identify them later."

"Yeah, but I don't think we need to broadcast that," Hannibal said, his eyes on Cindy's face. "In fact I think our best bet is to let the killer keep thinking he's got everybody fooled. We don't want to spook him."

"Agreed. We'll continue to pursue the missing person's case, and you follow up on any leads you get. And for God's sake keep me informed, because I'm on the line on this one with you. Will I be able to reach you at your office?"

"Actually, I've got a room at the Hyatt Regency in Reston. I'm going to work out of there to be closer to Great Falls. In the morning I'm going to see if I can get Monroe to talk to me."

"He's not dead." It was Cindy, who had crept very close to them while they talked. "There's no reason for Jason to be dead and there's no evidence that Jason is dead."

"They were very close," Hannibal told Rissik. "A lot more than just coworkers."

Rissik nodded. "Get the girl a decent dinner and get back on this in the morning, Jones. Got to protect the victims." His eyes wandered past Cindy quickly. "All the victims."


Hannibal drove Cindy back to her townhome on a quiet street only a block from the Potomac. He followed her inside and almost collided with her when she came to an abrupt halt in the center of the living room and muttered low.

"I thought I was out of this little cracker box."

Then she squared her shoulders and marched into the bedroom. Hannibal stayed behind, considering his woman's disappointment at not being able to hold onto the million dollar home she felt she deserved. Hannibal thought the little two-bedroom brick row house on the edge of Old Town had character. Cindy's subtle, if feminine decorating touches made the space hers. He admired the porcelain and crystal figurines that crowded shadow boxes, the mantle and nearly every other surface in the room. Lacy cloths covered tables at each end of her big chintz sofa. Victorian artwork graced the walls, filling the house with bright flowers, but were spaced to keep the rooms from looking cluttered. And there were the bowls of potpourri that added the scent of wildflowers. What was so awful about this cozy space? How much space does a single woman need?

Sooner than expected, Cindy huffed into the living room pulling a rolling overnight bag. Hannibal took it from her, collapsed the handle, and hauled it down to the car.

Traffic was light, yet by the time they made it to their hotel in Reston it was time for dinner. After getting settled in their room they moved to the hotel restaurant. If anyone recognized Hannibal from the tension at breakfast they made a point of not showing it. After searching in vain for something plain and simple on the menu, he settled on a chicken dish that featured a Portobello mushroom. Cindy seemed to enjoy the filet mignon that came with duck foie gras, asparagus and garlic whipped potatoes. Whipped, Hannibal guessed, because mashing was too good for them.

Despite the elegant surroundings Cindy was quiet and at times Hannibal felt her slipping away again. She emptied an atypical third glass of merlot before the meal ended.

When they returned to the room it was barely eight o'clock. The room was big, and very clean, but it smelled antiseptic, the way Hannibal always thought a sanitarium would smell. Cindy kicked off her shoes and began dropping articles of clothing as if she were alone.

"I am so sorry I got you involved in this," she mumbled, tossing her suit jacket into a chair.

"There's no reason to feel bad," Hannibal said, pouring water into the little coffeepot. "I needed a case, and I happen to like this particular client anyway."

"No, no, no." Cindy plunked down on the bed and began to unbutton her blouse. "I meant I'm sorry because of poor Jason. He'd be home watching TV right now if I hadn't called you in. The money would be gone but my friend wouldn't be missing."

Hannibal poured the heated water over a tea bag and moved slowly toward the bed. "How the hell did you come to that crazy conclusion?"

"It's not crazy," she said, sounding defiant despite her head hanging in front of her. "They weren't after Jason, you know. They were after this Irene bitch. If you hadn't gone to meet her they'd have just gunned her down and taken her away and they wouldn't have needed any cover-up. So they would have had no reason to ever go after poor Jason. Damn, I'm tired." She flipped her blouse in the general direction of her jacket. It fell a few inches short. Hannibal sat beside her on the bed.

"It's not physical fatigue, babe. You're emotionally exhausted, sort of like being in shock. The loss of your friend, the money, the murder, it's just hitting you hard. Take this and drink a little tea and you'll feel better."

"What's this? Drugs?" Cindy held her hand out, accepted the blue tablet, tossed it into her mouth and chased it with a swallow of tea before Hannibal answered.

"It's just to help you sleep. Unisom, over-the-counter, very mild."

"I don't feel like I need help falling asleep," Cindy said, unzipping her skirt and shimmying it down and off her without standing. "I just kind of feel like I'm all over the place. I'm a little confused right now. Except about one thing. Stop saying Jason is dead when you don't know."

"Cindy, honey, I don't want to hurt you." She leaned into him, her head landing against his chest. He wrapped an arm around her. "But the truth is, once this killer, whoever he is, decided to make Irene Monroe's death look like an escape, Jason's fate was sealed. Whether or not I was there, I'm convinced they were going to kill her, hide her, and set up a believable runaway scenario. For that picture to work, she had to run away with her boyfriend. They were not going to risk his showing up later to argue their theory."

"So, it would have worked anyway?"

"It would have worked better, babe." Hannibal lay back on the bed, pulling Cindy's head onto his chest. She curled against him like a child. "Cindy, if I hadn't been there to raise suspicion in a guy like Orson Rissik, they'd have never checked the car for prints. They'd have never looked for a bullet. They'd have never tested the sidewalk for blood."

"But they did," Cindy said, slurring just a bit. "So now it's better to have a hostage than be guilty of a second murder, right?"

Hannibal sighed, feeling her head move up and down with his chest. "Well, maybe when we find the person responsible we'll get more answers. That's why I want to confront George Washington Monroe, to see if I can get him to let something valuable slip."

"And to get my money," Cindy said. Hannibal chose not to reply and less than a minute later her breathing settled into a deeper, slower pattern. He waited a full five minutes before shifting her head to a pillow. Then he very slowly pulled back the covers on the other side of the bed and gently rolled her to it so he could cover her. Her face was still troubled, not the peaceful, innocent face he was used to waking up to from time to time.

Hannibal had no idea how to help her. She was hurting and she was angry, but he didn't fully understand why. He couldn't believe it was all about the money. The loss of her friend hurt, but was in no way her fault. And the dead woman was a complete stranger. Yet she was genuinely upset about something. But without understanding why, he couldn't do anything about it. He couldn't help her, but he couldn't just sit still either, and there was one thing he could do. He bent and kissed Cindy's cheek, barely touching her skin with his lips. Then he quietly eased the door open and slipped out.

In the car he checked to make sure his cell phone was on, in case Cindy awoke and found him gone. He hated to leave her alone, and Alexandria was a thirty minute haul down the beltway, but he had to pursue the case.

Hannibal had the platform to himself. He leaned back on his bench, arms crossed, waiting in silence. Still in his suit and shades he was almost lost in the darkness. A distant horn warned that a train was approaching. Its steel wheels sent vibrations ahead, down the rails and up through the wooden platform. Hannibal felt them but didn't react, even when Lane Stone walked up beside him.

"What on God's green earth are you doing out here?"

"Waiting for a train," he said, staring straight ahead. "Isn't that what people do out here?"

"Yeah, but they usually going someplace. You going someplace?"

"Meeting somebody."

"But you've already seen two trains come and go."

"Not sure what train they're on," Hannibal said. "But I know if I'm in the right place at the right time I can get my hands on the truth."

## -9-

Much of Hannibal's life came down to knocking on doors. Often they were the doors of affluent families in Northern Virginia who were victims of crimes. Sometimes they were the perpetrator of some swindle or crime that had made Hannibal's client a victim. This time he wasn't sure.

This particular morning he had left his woman still in restless sleep in the hotel room just before sunrise. Hannibal wasn't sure if George Washington Monroe would be willing to talk to him. If he refused to talk that would make Hannibal more suspicious. Monroe would know that. But if Monroe was willing to talk with him, Hannibal thought he might learn whether or not the man was capable of killing. Still, unannounced, he had driven to Monroe's huge colonial home on a quiet cul-de-sac surrounded by manicured lawns on a big enough lot to place all its neighbors at arms' length. As he walked up the steps to the front door the word stately came to his mind. It took him a moment to find the reference in his mind. Clearly this place reminded him of Wayne Manor. He didn't watch the Gotham television show, but he remembered the Batman TV show he had watched in reruns as a child.

The doorbell sounded like an entire orchestra of bells. Hannibal waited only ten seconds before a man in a neat blue suit opened the door. Hannibal wasn't sure what he expected, but it wasn't a white guy with wavy blond hair and horn rimmed glasses.

"Good morning," he said in an accent-free voice. "Is Mr. Monroe expecting you?"

"Probably. Tell him Hannibal Jones is here to discuss his wife's disappearance."

The stranger ushered him into the foyer and marched off through the house. Standing alone in the two story reception area he had time to notice the gleaming hardwood floors, crown molding, and the fact that the house seemed to smell of vanilla. The carpeted stairway to the second floor looked like a workout for any resident. He counted sixteen steps. When he looked down from the second level, the man who had greeted him at the door was standing beside him.

"Mr. Monroe requests that you join him in the sun room, where he is taking his morning coffee."

Hannibal followed his unnamed guide, who opened a door for Hannibal to enter. He walked across the white tile floor to stand beside a table almost covered by sections of the Washington Post, The New York Times and the Wall Street Journal. Seated at the table, in suit and tie, Monroe looked up from behind a piece of a newspaper. He looked at Hannibal for a moment as if deciding how to react to this guest. His sudden smile startled Hannibal when it flared up.

"Mr. Jones. Thank you for coming so early. I wasn't sure you had gotten my message."

"Excuse me?" Hannibal said. The doorman/personal assistant returned with a tray of sliced fruit and cheese and a pot of coffee. He filled mugs for the two men, and pulled Hannibal's chair out. The assistant left. Hannibal remained standing.

"I called your office and left a message but when you didn't call back I was concerned."

"I'm afraid I never did collect my messages," Hannibal said. "Are you saying you wanted to see me?"

"Of course," Monroe said, laying down the newspaper and sipping his coffee. "Please, have a seat."

Hannibal settled into his chair, tasted his own coffee and took a moment to enjoy the expansive view of Monroe's private garden in the early sunlight. He needed the moment to change his strategy. Monroe's obvious willingness to speak with him called for a shift in his approach. He decided to be direct.

"Mr. Monroe, I think you can understand my confusion here. You challenged me when we met at the police station. In fact you called me a liar to my face, and even accused me of having something to do with your wife's disappearance. Why did you want to see me?"

"Isn't it obvious? You're a detective, right? Well, I want to hire you."

Hannibal closed his eyes and sipped slowly. He needed to consider his next move very carefully. At that moment he was pursuing an investigation without an actual client, a dicey thing for a private detective to do. He had no justification to give the police for any digging he did, unless he was going to air Cindy's dirty laundry in public. Taking George Washington Monroe on as a client would make prying easier, and his local influence might make everything easier.

On the other hand, there were requirements that went along with a client-contractor relationship that could get messy if the client turned out to be a suspect. Well, one sticky item at a time.

"Your wife is dead, Mr. Monroe," Hannibal said over the edge of his cup. "Are you saying that you want her killer brought to justice?"

Monroe cupped his hands and dragged his face across his palms. When he looked up Hannibal wondered if any man could fake the kind of frustration mixed with grief that showed on Monroe's face.

"I know," Monroe said with a sarcastic sigh. "She looks like a trophy wife. Just the right accessory for a black man on the move, to ease his way into well-to-do white Southern society. I knew it looked that way when we married. Hell, she knew it, knew it from day one. I remember her saying to me that she would be a valuable asset, even if all she did was hold my arm and look cute. We laughed about it sometimes. But you need to know that wasn't the reason I married her. I loved Irene, Jones, but I know the husband is always the obvious suspect. The cops rarely move past the obvious. That makes you the most likely person to prove I didn't do it."

"So, you're telling me you're innocent," Hannibal said. Monroe responded with a warm, perfect smile, the kind that makes people like you whether they want to or not.

"No, I'm telling you I didn't kill Irene."

"I see. Do you know why I was meeting your wife in a lonely place at night?"

"As long as you were both dressed I don't really care," Monroe said.

"She was going to tell me about a business deal," Hannibal said, setting his coffee down. "A deal in which a very dear friend of mine lost a great deal of money. Are you going to plead innocent to that as well?"

Monroe's smile never wavered, but his eyes narrowed a little and his hands spread flat atop the bed of newspapers. "Perhaps I misunderstood you, Mr. Jones. Are you recording? Or are you being listened to? What crime are you investigating?"

"Not recording," Hannibal said, leaning back with his arms crossed. "Not wired, no mikes, no surveillance of any kind. And right now I'm only investigating the murder of a woman who trusted me. Anything else can wait."

Hannibal was surprised to hear himself say that. Of course a murder was more important than a swindle. A woman's life was more important than any amount of money. But not until he said it out loud did he realize that he had just put Cindy's problems behind the fate of a total stranger.

He only had a few seconds to consider his comment before Monroe snapped to his feet. "Let's take a walk in the garden."

Monroe led the way through French doors into what felt like a huge room with no ceiling, tastefully furnished with sculpted hedges and shrubs. A winding flagstone path led them past brown patches that Hannibal knew would be flowerbeds in a few months. Hannibal preferred the crisp, clean air of autumn to the flowery spring scents that always seemed to be trying to cover something up.

Their brief walk ended at a gazebo beside a stone fountain that was Hannibal's height. Hannibal thought this must be a most peaceful place to think, listening to the placid gurgling of the clear water splashing down out of the fountain. But he knew that the placid water sounds served a secondary purpose that morning. They gave George Monroe confidence that he was not being monitored.

"You want to frisk me too?"

Monroe leaned against the gazebo and turned on that same thousand watt smile. "Let's be real, okay? We're both hustlers. Different games, but both hustlers. We don't trust each other. Doesn't matter much to you, but I need you, so I'm trying to create a situation where we can maybe ease that a bit. It's easier if I know I'm only talking to you. So what can I do to make you trust me a little more?"

Hannibal could have asked Monroe a dozen questions about his finances, his relationship with his wife or his whereabouts on the night of the murder. But none of them would have fostered trust between them, and Hannibal had to admit to himself that if he was to find the truth, he needed Monroe's cooperation as much as Monroe needed him. Besides, it was more important to learn about the man than the facts of the case.

"Tell me how you met Irene."

Monroe stared for a moment, then nodded as if he understood Hannibal's motives. "We met at my alma mater, the University of Virginia, if you must know. They have asked me back a few times to speak to the students. I suppose I represent some sort of success picture for them."

"The kid who started with nothing and hit the big time," Hannibal said. "But that's not Irene's story, is it?"

"Oh, no," Monroe said, his eyes drifting off into the past. "Not at all. She was a trust fund baby. I went to UVA on a scholarship. She was studying art history. I had come through the School of Commerce. Finance was my area of concentration."

"I don't imagine you had too much in common."

"She was introduced to me at a little informal mixer after a talk I gave in the president's house," Monroe said, dropping onto the bench in the gazebo. "She had on this flowered sundress and her hair was halfway down her back. I told her I was knocked out by that Alabama accent. My people are from Tennessee."

"And yet you don't have any accent at all."

"That's right. I don't," Monroe said, staring into Hannibal's eyes. "And where are your people from, Jones?"

"Here and there. So she was a have and you were a have not, you were a bit older too, and there is the color thing. I'm sure she had an army of more suitable suitors. How did you manage to steal her away from them?"

Monroe placed his fingertips together and released a sigh from the back of his throat that sounded almost like a snake hissing. "She could see that I was truly and deeply in love with her. And I may have been a have not when I attended UVA but I sure wasn't when I returned. You see, I developed a talent early in life, Mr. Jones. A talent for turning a little money into a lot of money."

Hannibal could see that Monroe didn't like to be pushed. So he pushed just a little harder. "A valuable talent. Of course, first you have to get the little bit of money."

'Yeah, well I developed a talent for that too. Besides, I was a bit more mature than my Irene was. Like myself, she had already lost her parents. She needed guidance, she needed direction, and I supplied those things."

"Yes, you gave her direction and she provided you with a perfect entree into the society you wanted to be part of, in exchange for a very comfortable lifestyle, of course." Hannibal said, looking around at the private garden and impressive house. When he looked back Monroe was smiling again, fingers laced around one knee.

"Hannibal, do you know the expression, 'Git in where ya fit in?' Well I also have a talent for fitting in wherever I want to get in. Look around. You seen anybody out here looks like us? The population of Great Falls is about 9,000 but I doubt there are more than a hundred African Americans and most of them are maids, butlers or yard workers. It wasn't easy to get here, to get all this. I'm proud of what I've made of my life, but it don't mean much without my Irene. I need to know what happened to her, and why."

"And you figure if I work for you I'll be able to answer those questions for you."

"I know you will," Monroe said. "I did my homework, Mr. Jones. You don't quit, and if the mayor or some high level mobster or the President is the one responsible for Irene's death you'll bring him in. You're going to learn things, and I want to know what you know when you know it."

Hannibal stepped up into the gazebo and stared down at Monroe. "Okay, let me tell you what I know. I met your wife while on a case for a woman who is very special to me. That woman lost a great deal of money, her entire savings, in an investment scheme and your wife was going to tell me the details of that scheme. That gave whoever was running that scheme a damned good motive for killing her."

"And do you know that person was me?" Monroe asked, not wavering from Hannibal's fierce eye contact.

"I know that after you were married to her you raided Irene's trust fund and pretty much drained it dry. I know she found out. I know she hired people to investigate what happened to her money. I know you scared off a lawyer, chased off an accountant and bought off a private investigator to protect your secrets."

Monroe got to his feet, standing close enough for Hannibal to smash him to the ground but offering no defense. He somehow managed to look helpless and noble at the same time. "No denials from me. I ain't saying I'm a good man but I swear to God I didn't kill her, or have anything to do with her death. So help me."

The double meaning of those last three words threw Hannibal. After a moment he turned his eyes away. He was too close. He needed to get some distance, to see the case more broadly. He took a couple of steps up the path and turned back.

"My client wasn't the only person hurt in this scheme. There's no telling how many people have lost their savings. If one of them found out, they might have killed Irene to get at you."

Monroe took a deep breath and his smile returned. His Teflon shields were back up. "Look, I ain't saying I had anything to do with your client's tragic loss. But if you'll help me I'll replace all...however much money she may have lost in a bad investment."

So there it was. The devil's bargain was spelled out in black and white for him. Hannibal could recover Cindy's loss by simply taking a client and solving a murder. A very attractive trap indeed.

"I also know somebody went to a lot of trouble to make it look like she ran off with her boyfriend," Hannibal said, nibbling at the verbal bait. "He's also missing now and presumed dead. More motive for you. You admitted you knew all about them, and Irene told me you were having her followed."

Monroe took a few halting steps toward Hannibal. "Look at me. You can see that isn't my style. Besides, based on what you already say you know, wouldn't I try to chase him off or scare him off or buy him off first?"

When Hannibal grudgingly nodded, Monroe reached inside his guard and rested a hand on his shoulder. "If you're going to work for me there's no reason for me to lie, right? There's some sort of privilege, like with a lawyer. So if I was having my own wife followed, I could tell you. And there's no crime in that anyway. But I'm telling you now that I never did. Listen, do you like crème brule? I got some inside and it's so good with that Jamaica Blue coffee."

"I don't think Irene was just paranoid," Hannibal said. "I'm pretty sure the eyes she felt on her were real. So if you didn't have people watching her, is it possible these guys were really following you?" At that Washington shrugged, so Hannibal continued. "She told me they questioned Kevin Larson too. I understand he was your personal assistant for a while."

"Questioned Kevin?" Monroe started down the path toward the house, then turned and raised a fingertip toward Hannibal.

"Those guys might have been the FBI. They are very distrustful of a successful black man who comes from nothing. I know I've been a person of interest in some illegal business or other."

"Yeah, and your business partner, this Manuel Hernandez, has a pretty shady rep."

"Ex-partner," Monroe said, reaching for the door to the sun room. "He wasn't too bright. You've got to be careful when you're dealing in securities to stay out of those gray areas. But if a person were to wander into something like that, and if that person were a sharp operator, well, I'm sure that person would arrange things so all the suspicion would fall on somebody who's not too bright, like poor Manny." Monroe pulled the door open but Hannibal hesitated at the threshold.

"Interesting. So you're saying that if Irene knew anything of interest to the law, Hernandez would have a motive for keeping her quiet. Is that it, Monroe?"

Monroe turned and winked. "Hey, call me Wash. We're the partners now."

-10-

The Hyatt Regency had become the unofficial headquarters for the Irene Monroe murder case. Hannibal shared a lunch table in its restaurant with Cindy and Orson Rissik, who stared at his burger for a moment, wondering how to pick it up before deciding to cut it in half first.

"So what the hell's an Angus burger anyway? What makes it so special?"

"You got me," Hannibal said, picking up a quarter of his sandwich. "What makes a club sandwich worth 14 dollars?"

"The fact that we're eating in the wrong place. Now, did you make any progress questioning Monroe?" Rissik asked. "I need to have something solid pretty quick. I'm not getting much support back at headquarters."

"Actually, I did get some valuable info from Wash, or at least a few leads worth following up on."

"Wash?" Cindy asked. "What, you're old pals now? Is he no longer a suspect?" Cindy had declared that she needed a healthy meal so she was tackling a seafood salad with small, polite bites. Hannibal wondered if anyone really thought they ate lobster, scallops and shrimp for health reasons.

"He's still on the list," Hannibal said. "But that doesn't mean we can't be friendly. This way I can keep him close, just in case things do point to him in the end."

"Besides, he's an influential citizen around here," Rissik said between bites. "It's better to have the nasty camel inside the tent peeing out..."

"Wash won't cop to any wrongdoing, but he did tell me his old partner, Manny Hernandez, might have been under investigation by the FBI. If Irene Monroe had something on him that gives him a reason to want her dead."

"Unless he already talked to the FBI," Rissik said. "He might have had sense enough to cut a deal with the feds to drop it all on Monroe."

"Maybe you can check that out, Orson," Hannibal said. His sandwich really was pretty good, the herbs adding a nice tang to the moist grilled chicken breast. But then, he reasoned, there is only so much you can do with chicken, mayonnaise and a BLT. "I want to chase down this Kevin Larson who used to work for Wash. He might be able to give me an objective view of his relationship with Irene, and since he was probably also questioned by the FBI, maybe he can tell us how much Hernandez and Irene really knew."

"That sounds promising," Cindy said. "I'll join you."

Rissik glanced at Hannibal, and then focused on his food. Hannibal wished the lunch crowd was louder and more talkative.

"Honey, I'm better off doing this one alone."

Cindy chewed her salad slowly and thoroughly, allowing several seconds to pass before speaking again. "I can't just sit up in that room feeling sorry for myself, and I sure as hell can't go back to work. I have to stay with this. I have to do something."

Hannibal was unsure how strong he could be on this point, or how tender his reply needed to be. He was preparing his response when he felt a subtle nudge under the table.

"Hey, Jones, do you think Monroe is running a scam?" Rissik asked.

"I know he is," Cindy said with hatred dripping from her lips. "The man took me for every cent I had, and my poor Jason's too. Why do you think we're after him?"

Rissik managed to cloak his surprise. "Well if he's some sort of confidence man the FBI might not be the only agency watching him. There would be issues of hidden income."

"Sure," Hannibal said with a nod. "He may be a person of interest to the IRS as well. Or the SEC"

Rissik turned his attention to Cindy. "So, Miss Santiago, might you have some connections at Internal Revenue, or the Securities and Exchange Commission?"

"Hello. Business attorney," she said, pointing at herself. "I work with the IRS and the SEC on a daily basis."

"Then perhaps you can find out if either of those agencies has opened a case file on Monroe. He might have loved her, but men do strange things when they think they might be going to jail."

"Then it's settled," Hannibal said. "When we meet at dinner we'll all have something to report."

Finding Kevin and Vera Larson was no challenge for Hannibal. Information had a phone number for them in Falls Church, Virginia and connected him. "Vera Clean agency, this is Kevin, how can I help you."

Mr. Larson, my name is Hannibal Jones. I'm an investigator, looking into the disappearance of Irene Monroe."

"Damn shame," Larson said.

"Yes, well, I thought you might have some valuable background information. Can we get together?"

"Don't know what I can do, but I'd be happy to help," Larson said. "Come on over. You got a pen? I'll give you the address."

Larson's townhouse in Falls Church was an easy 20 minute drive down Route 7 in a community of two-level homes called Hillwood Square. Larson answered the door in a tee shirt, jeans and sneakers, and offered both a firm handshake and a ready smile.

"You're lucky to catch me at home," he said, waving Hannibal inside. "I have handyman work most days but it's unpredictable."

"I'm glad I caught you," Hannibal said, stepping inside. "I don't know what you might know about Irene..."

"I heard that Mrs. Monroe was missing and if I can be of any help at all, I'm happy to. She was always good to me and my wife."

Larson's complexion was polished mahogany, his hands strong and sure. He was in his early thirties and appeared fit, although he moved with a halting gait. Hannibal remembered a mention of a war wound.

"You spent some time in the military, I hear," Hannibal said, following Larson to the kitchen. The modest house was furnished with an eye to both cost and efficiency, but more JC Penney than Ikea. The kitchen carried the homey aroma of tomato sauce.

"Yeah, I was a corpsman in Afghanistan," Kevin said, stirring the sauce and turning the gas down.

Hannibal paused at a shadow box on the kitchen wall. "And proud of your service, I see. My dad was army so I don't know all the navy medals but…"

Kevin pointed with pride. "Navy Commendation Medal, Navy Achievement Medal, Meritorious Service, Good Conduct Medal, Expeditionary Medal, and the Afghanistan Campaign Service Medal. I was just a kid, but I was eager, you know. And they gave me my wish. Trained me up and sent me out there with the Marine Recon boys. I'm telling you, that was being alive, until I picked up a bit of shrapnel during a firefight. They fixed me up good but the limp never went away. I always thought that was one reason Wash hired me. We had something in common, you know?"

A dark-skinned whirlwind blew into the room carrying some sort of ledger. She dropped the book on the table, took a deep breath and spun to offer her hand.

"This is Vera," Kevin said, "the love of my life."

"Sorry if I'm a little distracted," Vera said. "The business don't run itself. You want something to drink?" Vera was dressed like Kevin, except that her jeans hugged her ample hips more tightly. She was darker than her husband and wore her hair in a natural style, pulled back by a wide headband. It reminded Hannibal of the Afro styles popular in 1970s. Her voice was so strong and confident he knew that people must often think she was being aggressive when she was just sure she was right.

"I got it," Kevin said, reaching for the refrigerator. Vera nodded and dropped onto a chair, opening her ledger and scanning for some information.

"I'll try not to take up too much of your time," Hannibal said, taking a seat beside Vera. "So Kevin, how'd you end up working for Wash?"

"Mostly luck," Kevin said, opening the refrigerator and pulling out a soda bottle. "I was kind of lost after the Navy cut me loose. I guess a gimp is no use in a war so they sent me home, but the medical training they give a corpsman doesn't get you a job. My mom couldn't stand to see me just sitting around. She used to work for Wash. She called him up and sent me over there and the next thing I knew, I was working for him."

While he talked, Kevin methodically pulled three glasses from a cabinet, filled them with ice and poured tea to within a quarter inch of the rim of each.

"Kind of a change from military service," Hannibal said when Kevin joined him and Vera at the table. "What was that like, being a personal assistant?"

"I got to tell you, it was pretty cool, and not so different from the Navy as you might think. All I had to do was run the house and take care of Wash's personal crap so he could focus on what he does."

"Which is?"

"Making money," Vera said without looking up.

"Seriously, that's his job," Kevin said with a laugh. "He finds investors and then just moves their money around and takes a cut when their investments grow. I don't understand the securities business or any of that business trading stuff, but I know he's damned good at it. And as long as I took care of him I had everything he had. I lived there with him, I ate like he ate and I drank like he drank. And of course there was Vera."

"She was already working there?" Hannibal sipped his drink and concealed a slight shiver. It was sweet tea, so sweet it made his teeth hurt. He put his glass down, hoping the ice would melt enough to water it down some.

"Yeah, she was Irene's assistant."

"I was supposed to make her appointments and take care of her monstrous wardrobe and so on," Vera said with a wry smile. "Truth is, I was more of a paid friend."

"And a confidante," Hannibal said. "I'll bet you knew her better than anyone."

"Mm-hm. I sure thought I did. But I just can't believe she would up and leave that man. Can't swear she loved him, but she sure loved her life."

"And how about you? Were you as happy there as Kevin?"

She put down her pen and turned her flashing eyes on Hannibal. "They was good to me, so yeah, I liked the job, even before I met this big lug."

Hannibal turned to Kevin. "And you fell for her."

"Like a ton of bricks, man," Kevin said. "And we was quite a team, taking care of the Monroes."

"How about them?" Hannibal asked, leaning back. "Were they a team?"

Kevin took a long drink, sipping slowly. It was the kind of pause Hannibal often saw when someone wasn't prepared for a question and wanted to choose the right answer.

"Honestly, I thought they were the dream couple," Kevin finally said. "They seemed so in love. I'm with Vera, I can hardly believe Irene would run off like that."

"What if she didn't?"

"What do you mean?"

"What if she didn't leave of her own free will?" Hannibal asked.

Kevin mulled that for a second. "What, you mean like a kidnapping? I guess Wash has enough money to make it worth it."

Hannibal nodded. There was a possibility no one else had mentioned. He wondered why Wash hadn't asked about that.

"A possibility. But we think she may have come to harm."

"What?" Kevin's brows rose. "Why would anybody want to hurt Irene?"

"That's what I was hoping you could tell me. Mrs. Larson, you talked with Irene every day. Do you think she might have known anything, had any information that might be important enough to kill for?"

"I can't imagine what that might have been," Vera said. "We had some men come around asking questions a while back, but I never knew what they was after. Kev, check that sauce, would you?"

"We're just trying to figure out if anyone might benefit from her death."

Kevin went to the stove and stirred the sauce. "That don't make no sense. Nobody benefits if she's gone. It's not like somebody gets an inheritance or something."

"Didn't she have money of her own?"

Vera laughed. "It ain't public knowledge, but that man took all her money."

It appeared that they did talk about everything. Hannibal had to think that if Irene had valuable information, then the Larsons would be in danger as well.

"You knew their lives pretty well," Hannibal said. "I bet you both knew about Irene's boyfriend." Kevin sat down and the couple looked at each other before turning to Hannibal and nodding. "If there was somebody else in Wash's life, you would know, right?"

Both the Larson's looked down. Kevin took a drink and averted his eyes. Vera laid her hands flat on the table. "Mr. Monroe, he had nobody else in his life, Mr. Jones. No family, no children, no real friends, nobody. He had lots of parties and he had lots of people he did business with, but he was a lonely man, Mr. Jones. Irene was all he had, except for us."

During the momentary pause Hannibal could hear a couple arguing next door. Vera looked back down at her ledger. Everyone took a drink, ice tinkling in their glasses. Despite its sweetness Hannibal thought the tea smelled bitter.

"His was a small world, and yet he fired you both."

"Not really," Kevin said. "Wash just kind of thought we needed to move on to better things. He staked me all the equipment to get my handyman business going. I hated to go but I sure couldn't turn away from the opportunity."

"And you, Mrs. Larson. Were you equally sorry to go?"

Vera glanced at her husband before answering. "I was so happy there, Mr. Jones. But Mr. Monroe offered to set me up in this cleaning business. I couldn't say no. Besides, those men had just been around asking all those questions. I was glad to get away from that at least."

Hannibal looked around at the Larson home, less than a quarter of the square footage of the house up in Great Falls, and thought he knew the limits of Monroe's generosity. Hannibal wasn't sure why Monroe had sent the Larsons away, but he had bought their absence, and their loyalty, at discount rates.

"I still miss hanging with Wash, though," Kevin said. "He was like family to me. If somebody really did hurt Irene, I sure hope you find them and make them pay."


Dinner was a lot noisier than lunch had been, but Orson Rissik looked a good deal happier. Cindy at least didn't complain out loud. Hannibal just wanted to eat and move on. He had more in mind to get done before the night ended.

Seating was close in Ruby Tuesday on a Friday night. It was a little too warm for the suit and tie Hannibal still wore, and he could smell the fried food at the next table. But despite the volume of diners they didn't wait nearly as long to be served as they had at lunch. He pulled one of the wings out of their shared appetizer sampler and turned to Rissik.

"So tell us, oh connection to mainstream law enforcement, what did Fairfax County's finest learn today?"

"It will come as no surprise to you that the investigation developed nothing new today," Rissik said, biting into a spring roll. "But before I go into how my afternoon went, I think we should let the lady speak."

"Why thank you, kind sir," Cindy replied as a waitress placed a plate in front of her. "It's nice to dine with gentlemen. Even here."

"And yet," Hannibal said, "you managed to snatch up the last piece of fried mozzarella before the entrees arrived. So, you spoke with your contacts in those big government agencies in charge of keeping me from having any money. What did they have to say?" He popped the last bit of wing into mouth. They were labeled fire wings, but weren't nearly hot enough for his tastes.

"The SEC was a bust," Cindy said. "If they have a file open on George Washington Monroe, nobody knows about it."

"They're wimps. What about the IRS?"

Cindy leaned in close to the table. "None of this is for public release, but I was able to confirm that the IRS is building a case against Monroe. The way it was explained to me, they think it's pretty obvious that something shady's going on, but the situation is so convoluted that it will take them some time to unravel the ball of yarn we call Monroes fiscal picture. . Hmmm. This grilled salmon is surprisingly good."

"So if the wife had the kind of evidence that could save the feds months of work, that might have given Monroe a motive," Hannibal said, "Or even the dropped partner, Hernandez." He shook some hot sauce on his ribs and took another bite. That was better.

"I don't know," Rissik said, sipping his iced tea. "Hernandez might be off the hook. My guy at the Bureau says they definitely had a sit down with him. They don't want to talk about what they got out of him but if he was interviewed by the FBI you got to figure they cut some kind of a deal or he'd be in jail right now, which he ain't."

"Have they talked to anybody else?" Cindy asked.

"He wouldn't give me that much, but I was able to confirm that they did not talk to the wife." Rissik sat behind a sirloin accompanied by broccoli and a baked potato—again.

Cindy stared down into her food, pulling another small bite off with her fork. "If they indict him on fraud charges, or any kind of business irregularities they'll freeze his assets."

Rissik looked at Hannibal who tried hard not to react at all. It seemed an inappropriate remark when the two men were focused on the murder, and Hannibal figured she thought so too. That was the reason she never looked up after saying it.

Hannibal quickly reported on his interview with the Larsons. The rest of the meal passed quietly. After a brief tug-of-war over the bill, which Hannibal won, Rissik headed home and Hannibal walked Cindy back to their hotel room.

The hotel was barely a block away. An autumn breeze was pushing out of the parks on their left as they began their stroll down Presidents Street. Fallen leaves rustled around their feet. On the way they passed a trail into the park that Hannibal thought would be a good starting point for a morning run. As they crossed Market Street, halfway to the Hyatt Regency, Cindy took Hannibal's arm. It felt a little forced, but her spirits really did seem brighter, as if the fog she had been lost in was lifting. Right then he wished the hotel was a little farther away.

They went up to their room in what felt like a purposeful silence. Cindy slipped off her shoes as soon as she was inside, stripped to her bra and panties, and sat on the bed. Hannibal turned the television to News Channel 8 and stretched out beside her. Cindy slowly leaned over so that her head rested on his chest.

"You are so sweet, Hannibal. I think you hate being with a news junkie."

"Not at all, babe," Hannibal said, resting a hand on her hip. "I just want you to relax."

Cindy snuggled against him. She kissed his chest and started unbuttoning his shirt. Her hair cascaded across his body, hanging down to the bed. His fingertips slowly stroked her naked thigh. Her perfume reached up to him, trying to pull him into the right mood. But she was moving very slowly. Despite her seductive actions, he sensed an underlying tension that would not allow for a truly romantic mood. She raised her head, still not speaking or looking at him. When she tugged at his belt he squeezed her waist with one hand.

"You don't have to, you know."

Cindy's head dropped onto his stomach. "I'm sorry. I'm not very convincing, am I?"

Hannibal took her shoulder and eased her back until her face was beside his.

"I'm on a case, baby. You don't need to be the femme fatale tonight."

Cindy's lips clenched and Hannibal feared she might tear up. "I know. It's just that we so rarely have time together like this, and this place is so nice. I feel like we're wasting the hotel room."

Hannibal didn't know what to say, and he realized that the feeling was becoming familiar. He held her close, wishing he knew the magic incantation to make his woman's unhappiness float away. Instead they sat quiet, watching the local news go by for a while. As Cindy became more and more relaxed Hannibal focused on shoving his natural impatience to the back of his mind. After her head drooped and snapped back up she looked up to him.

"Honey, I think I want to go to sleep a little early. Do you mind?"

"Of course not," Hannibal replied, "but my work day isn't over yet. You put this case out of your mind and get some rest and when I get back, we'll see whether or not we'll waste this room."

Seated on that bench under the stars at the train station, Hannibal's mind was not on Cindy Santiago's seductive form. Nor was it on her missing money, or even the murder he was determined to solve. He was only remotely aware of the sharp breeze that cut through the night every few minutes, or the tumultuous racket generated by an army of crickets on the other side of the tracks. He wasn't thinking of anything, really. He was just waiting.

Waiting was not something he learned to do during his half-dozen years as a New York City cop. Those years had taught him determination, intimidation, observation and deduction. It was his time with the Secret Service that taught him to wait. Some days he spent hours staring at a crowd in the streets or at an airport or even a train station like that one in Alexandria, waiting for something that he didn't expect. Those times were sort of like shutting himself down without sleeping. His senses were alert while the rest of him slipped into stasis, hibernating until other systems were needed.

People came and went, most of them unaware that Hannibal was even there. He was practically invisible in his black suit, and he removed his sunglasses to be less conspicuous. As midnight approached, so did the last train of the evening. It was his last chance of the day to see what he was looking for. If his quarry wasn't aboard he would go home and return tomorrow.

The platform vibrated as the giant steel machine approached. The vibration increased, the rhythmic pounding of the drive wheels becoming more and more insistent until the train pulled in. Then came the orgasmic squealing as the brakes locked the wheels in place, and the final explosive huff of steam indicating that the behemoth had collapsed, exhausted until the engineer stoked it up again in thirty minutes.

Passengers disembarked and a handful moved to board. Hannibal screened them as they passed, ignoring women, children and men over a certain age. One figure caught his attention. The man wore a suit and carried a black overnight bag. He was tall and gaunt, with light brown or blonde hair. He walked into the station. After a few seconds, Hannibal stood and followed.

The station was almost empty, so Hannibal stayed at the door until his quarry reached the opposite entrance. Even in the well-lit station the stranger could have been mistaken for Jason Moore from across the room. His tan suit was crumpled from being slept in on the train, but it was expensive enough to belong to a lawyer.

It could have been Jason himself, if not for the half inch of red ink poking up out of his collar.

When the stranger stepped into the night, Hannibal moved quickly across the station. The tall stranger had already crossed the parking lot and was moving down the street as quickly as he could without running. Of course, he was dragging a suitcase. Even walking at his normal aggressive pace Hannibal was slowly closing the gap. The clack of the stranger's oxfords on the cement became an echo of Hannibal's own.

The stranger crossed the street and continued down the dark sidewalk, not looking left or right. Hannibal walked as if they just happened to be going the same way, enjoying the crisp night air filling his lungs more as the walk stretched into the second block. Once they left King Street there was no one on the street but the two of them. The half-moon shed little light, but presented a lovely sight hanging over the short buildings of the part of the city still called Old Town. These three or four story structures were mostly commercial-residential hybrids, storefronts with apartments above.

Three blocks from the train station, the stranger put the suitcase down and pulled a key out of his pocket. Hannibal kept walking while the stranger unlocked the driver's door of an older, dark sedan. Hannibal was within ten feet of him when he looked up.

"So what I want to know is, did they pay you enough to risk jail time for kidnapping and murder?"

In the dim light the stranger's eyes narrowed, then widened and his mouth dropped open. Hannibal read the entire internal monologue on his face. Who is this guy? What does he want? What is he talking about, kidnapping and murder? Did those guys set me up to be the fall guy for some crime?

The stranger's fingers failed him. The sound of the keys hitting the sidewalk seemed to shock him into action but by the time he turned to run Hannibal already had a hand down the back of his collar and was swinging him to the side. The stranger grunted as Hannibal smashed him into the side of the car and held him in place with an elbow thrust against his spine.

"I figured they hired local talent for their little game. Didn't you know you were a decoy, sent as evidence that their victim left town?" Hannibal asked while he quickly patted the man down. As expected, he was not armed. He flipped the man's wallet open and scanned his driver's license. "So, Walter, did you think it was some sort of practical joke or something? Did it never occur to you that you were meant as evidence that the guy they killed was still alive somewhere?"

"I don't know nothing," Walter said, whining and stammering at the same time. "They just told me to get on the train with the girl and ride to the end of the line."

"Yeah, well you'll have your chance to tell your story to the cops," Hannibal said. Crouching quickly he scooped up the dropped keys. He tossed them onto the roof of the car, backed up and drew the Sig Sauer P220 from under his right arm. Holding his pistol casually at his side he said, "Get in the car, stupid. I don't want to hurt you, but if you try to run, trust me, you'll just die tired."

It took Walter a while to unlock the door because of the way his hands were shaking, but once he got it open he slid onto the seat. Hannibal slammed the door shut and walked around to get in the other side. It was a cool night, but that didn't stop the beads from popping out on Walter's forehead.

"Start her up and pull a U-turn," Hannibal said. "We're going back to the train station. And meanwhile, you can tell me who gave you the suit and told you to get on that train."

"It was the girl," Walter said, driving slowly, glancing often at the gun on Hannibal's lap. "Lucinda. We used to hang out sometimes. She brought me the suit and said I could make two hundred dollars just for taking a ride with her. Times have been tough so I figured, why not? Nothing illegal about taking a ride, right?"

"And where is this Lucinda now?" Hannibal asked as they pulled into the train station parking lot.

"Who knows? She got off up in Canada. She wasn't from around here anyway. Me, I hate the cold, so I just turned around and came home. I should have stayed in The City. I got family in Yonkers."

Hannibal signaled Walter to get out and walked him to the black Volvo. Hannibal's instincts told him that the lead he had waited in the dark for was turning out to be a dead end. Walter was just a hustler. He never even met the killer or whoever set up the fake disappearance. Lucinda with no last name was the person Hannibal needed to talk to, but unlike Walter, she probably had sense enough to lay low for a while. Or maybe she was from Canada and was happy to have somebody else pay her way home. Either way, he had little hope of finding her.

When they reached Hannibal's car Walter stopped, his eyes moving between Hannibal's face and the pistol held in the shadow of his suit coat. He almost looked as if he was going to cry. Hannibal shook his head. What had happened to cheap thugs in the last few decades? The guys in the Shadow paperbacks and Batman comics Hannibal read as a kid were a different breed. Those guys would have kicked this guy out of the union.

"Relax Walter, I'm not taking you for a ride, at least not in the old movie sense. I am going to call a good cop I know who, as I think of it, won't want to be hassled at this time of night with business. I'll leave you in his care for the night. Now that I think of it, him you should be afraid of."

# -11-

# SATURDAY

Hannibal always woke up first. He had been an early riser all his life, from the days he wanted to see his dad leave in his uniform every morning. So he was startled when he opened his eyes and found himself alone.

He didn't have to look far. Cindy was curled up in the chair over by the window, wrapped in the spare blanket, softly backlit by the morning sun. Her hair was a matted mess. One of her tiny feet poked out from the bottom of the blanket. Her scent reached out to him, something by Hermes whose actual name he couldn't pronounce right. It smelled of vanilla and jasmine and made his heart ache when she wore that little girl face. Her face was turned down, her lower lip poking out, and she looked up at him from under her eyebrows.

"I don't understand," she said.

Hannibal sat up in the bed. "What, baby? What don't you understand?"

"What's wrong with me?"

Hannibal wasn't sure if she was asking a question or making a statement, so he left enough silence for her to fill it in.

"I've been up since four. I always sleep well. How can I feel so restless and drained at the same time? Am I going crazy?"

"No, sweetheart, you're just a little down. You've had a couple of pretty terrible blows. Lost a good friend."

"Maybe," Cindy said, with more hope than certainty in her voice.

"Okay," Hannibal said, not wanting to argue the point, "But you've also had the rug yanked out from under you financially. I know you had some great plans and they've just been derailed."

"But that doesn't happen to me," she said through clenched teeth. "My God, I grew up with no mother, learned English at the same time my father did, but still this skinny Puerto Rican girl got into law school and graduated third in her class. My plans don't..." There was a long pause. "Don't get derailed."

"Sorry to say it, baby, but it happens to everybody," Hannibal said. He kept his voice soft but his words stayed strong. "The rest of us are used to things not going our way, but you're not. Truth is, you're a bit spoiled, babe." He said it with a smile, but realized he had never had that exact thought until just then. Cindy's eyes went down and to one side.

"But things do go your way," Cindy said, shaking her head. "We all knew the guy witnesses saw get on that train to Canada wasn't Jason. But you knew it was somebody hired locally. And you knew the killer wouldn't tell him why he was taking that trip. So he had no reason to stay away, and you knew he'd want to come home when the job was done. It all seems so obvious when you look at it after the fact."

"Most mysteries do," Hannibal said. He wanted to ask why they were talking about that at all. "And I had the advantage of experience. I've chased a lot of runaways."

Cindy clenched her eyes tight, then looked up at Hannibal, on the edge of tears. "How do you do that? How can you always be so sure?"

He shrugged. "I don't know. Maybe because I've been right enough to count, and so far being wrong hasn't killed me. Maybe because most of the time doing anything is better than doing nothing. Maybe just because for me, doubt is a killer. And you know what else is a killer? Hunger."

He grabbed the phone beside the bed and pushed a button. When he heard a response he ordered a pot of strong coffee and a three-egg omelet with ham, peppers, onions, mushrooms and Monterey jack cheese. Then he looked at Cindy with raised eyebrows. Her mouth hung open a bit and her blink rate increased. He couldn't remember seeing indecision on her face, especially over something so simple.

"Yeah, make it two," he said into the phone. "And throw on some toast. Thanks."

When he hung up, Cindy asked, "What will you do today?"

"Well, I'll want to see if Rissik got anything else out of Jason's stand-in," Hannibal said. "He'll be pissed about working this on a Saturday so he might shake something loose. And I'm going to see if I can get face to face with Hernandez. I need to get a sense of whether he had a motive to off Irene. While I'm doing that, you're going to a spa and getting a massage and whatever treatment will make you relax for a while. But before any of that, I'm going sit here with my lady and have some breakfast. Now quit acting like a victim and drag that cute little ass back over here into this bed."

He stared at her until she moved. Her knees straightened like old rusty hinges but she finally stood and walked over to join him.

Columbia Heights is a neighborhood still searching for itself. Situated in Northwest Washington DC it once aspired to be upscale, but somehow got stuck being a densely packed collection of condominiums and townhouses. Leaning against Howard University, it was a Black neighborhood until the riots that followed Martin Luther King's murder. It holds both the Ecuadoran embassy and the Mexican Cultural Institute so some people think of it as a Latin neighborhood. George Washington Monroe was among them.

"Not hard to guess why Manny decided to buy a club up here," Monroe said from the passenger seat of Hannibal's car. "He can get lost in the shuffle real easy. He always wanted to be invisible. I always wanted to be famous. That's a lot of what pulled us apart business-wise."

"Or, maybe he just couldn't take your pompous attitude," Hannibal said, driving slowly down the narrow street. "Look more closely and you'll see that half the neighborhood's black. Maybe half of the rest are Latin."

"Well, okay, I haven't been here in a while, but it looks like you might be right. Wonder where they all went."

"It's a lot cheaper to live in Prince George's County over in Maryland," Hannibal said. Still he couldn't deny there were plenty of Hispanic faces on the street, and every one reminded him how he had hated to leave Cindy alone that morning. He was worried about her, but knew that his best chance at making her feel better was to get to the bottom of the Jason's murder. At least, he thought so.

Getting into the District had been an easy half hour's drive, a few miles down Route 7 and over to the George Washington Parkway. Once they got onto the Key Bridge they left Virginia behind for the streets of Washington. In this case, they were a bewildering collection of narrow, traffic-packed streets named for numbers, letters and states in no perceivable pattern. In the process they even drove past the restaurant from which Cindy had darted into traffic and started this case. There were lots of pedestrians on the street, which had prompted his slow pace and their conversation.

On the way Monroe had explained the long string of phone calls that had led him to his old partner, Manny Hernandez. Apparently he had bought, and was managing, a club on M Street that alternated between soul food and Mexican food, with a hip hop DJ some nights and Salsa on others. In a multi-cultural city, in a neighborhood known for its ethnic diversity, it made a kind of sense.

Hannibal found a parking space near the Metro station and accepted it as the closest they would get to their destination. A large construction site loomed across the street. Hannibal tried to move on, but Monroe stopped and appeared to be admiring the work being done.

"Got a fascination with real work?" Hannibal asked.

Wash pointed from left to right at the work area. "Jones, this is one of my favorite achievements. When we worked together,

Manny and I put together much of the financing for this project. It's called DC USA."

"Real catchy, Wash. A mall, I take it."

"A retail complex," Monroe said. "More than 546,000 square feet of shopping pleasure. There's going to be a Target at that end and a Best Buy down there and lots more in between. And the most important thing is what this area needs most, lots and lots of underground parking. This, my friend, is a guaranteed money maker that will benefit the neighborhood."

"I'm not one of your marks, Wash," Hannibal said, tugging Monroe by the arm, "and I'm also not your friend. Let's go find Hernandez."

Taberna Pacifico didn't open until five but the staff was already setting up for a busy night. The door was unlocked so Hannibal walked in with Monroe close behind. Heavy drapes gave the wide dining area a cavernous gloom and even hours before dinner the air was cluttered with a chaos of spices that assaulted Hannibal's nose. They walked toward the back of the house until a grim-faced man stepped into their path. His slicked-back black hair was thinning but not his waist. He looked to Hannibal like a retired Mexican wrestler, one of those guys who wears a fancy mask when he's doing his work. Hannibal stopped at a polite distance but Monroe surged ahead.

"We're here to see Manny," Monroe said, offering a broad, persuasive smile. "We'll only be a minute."

The bouncer was right in Monroe's face but, to his credit, Monroe didn't even blink. He met the bouncer's hard look with the same disarming smile he had shown Hannibal the day before. Then he took another step toward the back.

The clatter of dishes in the kitchen almost cloaked the low rumble coming from the bouncer's chest but Hannibal heard it. The bouncer presented a palm, which Monroe tried to step around. The bouncer's right fist cocked back, but Hannibal's gloved right hand stopped it mid-swing. The two men locked eyes.

"You don't want none of this," Hannibal said in a low, hard voice. "Walk away."

Hannibal's arm began to shake as he kept the bouncer's fist from moving forward. He knew what happened next and every scenario he imagined ended with the other man's knee dislocated or his own nose broken or both. But then a strident voice came from the back room.

"What the hell? Is that Wash?"

Monroe rushed past the bouncer toward a man who could have been his mirror image except for his obvious Latin background. Same height, weight and build. Same disarming smile, but Hernandez had not aged as well as Monroe. If his life was made into a movie, Ricardo Montalban would have been cast to play Hernandez.

"Manny, you crafty old bastard," Monroe said, moving with all the speed he could muster while hampered by his limp. He was grinning like the unpopular kid at his high school reunion, not wanting to remind the others how they treated him back then.

"Wash, you son of a bitch," Hernandez said, but he wasn't smiling. His right cross caught Monroe on the side of his jaw, tossing him backward to land flat on his back on a dinner table.

That was all the guidance the bouncer needed. His huge left fist whipped around toward Hannibal's face. Luckily for him, Hannibal had already formed an alternative mental picture that did not involve dislocation. He ducked under the sweeping left hook and reached down to grab the cuffs of the man's pants. When he snapped upright the bigger man's feet were yanked out from under him. The average man might have cracked his skull open on the floor, but this man was a wrestler. He knew how to fall, absorbing the impact with his arms, and rolled to his feet. Now Hannibal had some distance and could figure to use his kick boxing skills to put the man down without permanent damage to either of them. If he had to.

"We don't want this, Mr. Hernandez," Hannibal said while keeping his eyes on the bouncer. "Just want to talk. If not me, it will be the police because you'll be a suspect in the murder investigation."

"Murder? What murder?" His accent was cultivated and Hannibal imagined he was unbeatable in his day at charming the ladies.

Monroe sat up on the table, all the fight knocked out of him. "Manny, someone's gone and killed Irene. I'm not accusing you, but your name is going to come up, old buddy, so we need to talk."

Hernandez considered for a few seconds, then gestured to his bouncer to relax and waved Monroe inside.

"He comes with me," Monroe said, pointing toward Hannibal. Hernandez nodded and the three walked back through the kitchen to a small square office tucked into the back. The desk filling much of the room was cluttered with stacks of small bills, receipts and an adding machine. Smoke curled up from an ashtray embedded in the clutter, from a cigar that someone had not quite extinguished. There were only two chairs and Hernandez settled into the one behind the desk. Monroe took the other. Hannibal stood by the door. The smell of cigar smoke seemed out of place to him in a restaurant.

Hernandez picked up the stub of his cigar and thrust it at Monroe.

"You fucked me over good, Wash," Hernandez said. "I saw how you arranged the whole setup. The feds were already sniffing around and the way the paper trail read, all the stink was going to stick to me."

Monroe sat up a little straighter as if to take the shots fairly, but he didn't respond. Everyone in the room seemed to know that this wasn't what the conversation was about. Hernandez glanced at Hannibal, stared for a moment at Monroe, then looked at his shoes.

"So Irene is dead?"

"Yeah," Wash said, just loud enough to be heard.

"I'm sorry," Hernandez said. "Murdered?"

"Gunned down in the street," Monroe said, hooking a thumb at Hannibal. "He saw it."

"You don't think it was me?"

"Your opening statement would seem to point toward motive," Hannibal said.

"My beef's with Wash," Hernandez said. "Irene was a sweet girl. I had no reason to wish her harm."

Hannibal looked to Monroe but when he remained silent, Hannibal continued. "She knew a lot about the way you and Wash did business. Somebody might think she knew the kind of stuff that would put you behind bars. Somebody might think you needed to shut her up to cover your ass."

"Well, somebody would be an idiot," Hernandez said, getting to his feet. "First of all, I don't play that way and Wash knows it. We always got what we needed without guns or knives. The good Lord gave me the gift of the silver tongue and it's all I've ever needed to stay ahead of trouble. Besides, the feds already know everything that might have got me trouble." He turned to Wash. "They know, cause they got it all from me."

Hannibal noticed that Hernandez was an exception among Latin men he knew. Instead of intensifying as he became more emotional, his accent faded. Monroe blinked in apparent astonishment.

"You sold me out to the feds?"

"You fucked me over good, Wash,"

"Come on, Manny," Monroe said. "We both know what we are. It's how you play this game. We stood face to face."

"Yeah, we did. You made a good move to protect yourself. I made the best move I had. I cut a deal with the IRS. They were happy to have the dirt I gave them on you, and it put me in the clear. It'll still take them years to put together a case on you. I gave up a lot, but I didn't give them everything."

Monroe looked down and after a minute he said, "Thanks."

"And I really am sorry about Irene."

For a brief moment Hannibal was afraid they were going to hug.

"Let's go Wash. If this guy had no motive for killing Irene, we got no reason to be here. We don't need to let the trail get any colder."

Monroe nodded to Hernandez but they didn't shake hands. Hannibal stayed close to him on the way out, keeping his eyes on the bouncer. Back in his car Monroe was silent as they took off. He shook his head, then nodded, as if he were having a conversation with himself. Hannibal tapped buttons on his steering wheel and vintage Isaac Hayes burst from the speakers. He hadn't selected a song, but once "Ain't No Sunshine When She's Gone" had started, he thought it would be worse to cut it off.

"She's really gone," Monroe said during the instrumental section. "It didn't seem real until I told Manny. It wasn't the truth until I said it out loud."

"You got a funny relationship with the truth," Hannibal said.

"Yeah, we ain't exactly friends," Monroe said. "Maybe I ought to see her more often."

Hannibal steered unhurried toward I-395 to break free of The District. "Her?"

"The truth," Monroe said. "Is there any doubt the truth is a woman? She's so stubborn, and yet so changeable. So beautiful, especially when you see her naked."

"Hernandez was wrong. You're the one blessed with the silver tongue. You got any particular truths you want to face today?"

Monroe took a deep breath, and Hannibal suddenly felt as if he had been set up for something. "Yeah. Yeah there is. Are you rushing someplace?"

Hannibal wanted to get back to Cindy, not just to have dinner with her, but because he didn't want her to spend too much time alone right then. He wanted to touch base with Rissik to evaluate what he got out of Walter. And he wanted to see if there was a way to learn all that Hernandez had told the IRS.

"No, no hurry."

"Good," Monroe said. "Take me there. Take me to the place where it happened. Right now, that's the only truth I need to face."

Shadows were long by the time Hannibal pulled into the shopping center parking lot. There were few people walking in the area, and only a couple cars scattered around the lot. That was all probably good news for Wash Monroe's public image.

Monroe had asked Hannibal to stop at a VABC store, where he picked up a bottle of cognac and a wine cooler. He poured out the cooler before getting back into the car and with a very steady hand half-filled the bottle with Courvoisier. He offered the small bottle to Hannibal, who declined. During the drive Monroe sipped at the bottle until it was empty, and then refilled it to the halfway mark.

When they climbed out of the car Hannibal was impressed by Monroe's steadiness. He may have needed liquid support to face the truth, but he did it without showing any obvious signs of intoxication. Hannibal walked to the spot where he had watched the murder. He waved a hand toward the spot in front of him where Irene Monroe had crumpled at his feet. There was no mark, no stain, no sign or indication. But he knew it was the spot.

Monroe stared at the place Hannibal indicated and took a deep breath, as if inhaling the moment, as if he could smell the horrific event that took place there. He didn't look left or right, and Hannibal wondered what it was he thought he saw there. If he stared long enough would he see who did it, or why? Not likely. But standing a foot away from Wash Monroe, separated only by the place the man's wife fell, Hannibal was finally certain that he did not kill her.

"Did she know?" Monroe asked after a minute of silence.

"You mean, know who it was?"

"No," Monroe said with a bitter smile. "Did she know what happened? Did she know she was dead?"

"It was sudden and unexpected," Hannibal said. "I guess, well probably not. She probably never knew what happened."

"I think I want to go get drunk. Would you like to get drunk, Mr. Jones?"

"I think you're doing fine for both of us," Hannibal said. "Maybe you should get some food in you."

"That is only a good idea if you will sit with me. Now, that tavern at the end of the block there serves an excellent crab cake, and has both Guinness Stout and Founder's Breakfast Stout on tap."

The crab cakes did turn out to be good, and Hannibal washed them down with a good draft beer. He was unfamiliar with Founder's Stout but when the bartender told him it was brewed with flaked oats, Kona coffee and chocolate he had to try it. He was not disappointed.

Monroe also ate, but he kept the cognac flowing quickly enough to offset the effects of a good meal. As the room began to fill with the early shift of Saturday night regulars, Hannibal hoped Monroe had eaten enough at least to keep from getting sick. His and Monroe's were the only dark faces in the little corner bar, and he had no desire to draw everyone's attention.

The place featured oak plank flooring and dark wood furniture and decor that seemed to absorb what little light there was. Spilled spirits had soaked into the tables and probably the floor to release a subtle aroma that probably made men feel that drinking too much was expected. Sports on two different televisions combined with random conversations to become one big white noise generator. Hannibal sat on the edge of his chair with his back to the bar, facing the only entrance and exit. He had done protection details in places just like this. It was his idea of a great place to drink, but a terrible place to have to work. He watched Monroe upend another glass.

"So, any more truth you want to face?"

A new glass landed beside Monroe's elbow and he raised it as if in tribute. "Charles Ponzi," he said, taking a drink. "Do you know what a Ponzi scheme is, Hannibal?"

"Well, sure," Hannibal said, sipping his beer. "It's a financial plan that offers abnormally high short-term returns to entice new investors. The high profits a Ponzi scheme pays require an ever-increasing flow of money from new investors to keep the scheme going. The person running the scheme pays Peter with the new investment money from Paul."

Monroe nodded as if imparting great wisdom to an initiate. "At the turn of the century, the last century, Charles Ponzi came to this country from Italy with nothing but the shoes on his feet. He was a genius and smooth as polished brass. The greatest swindler in American history. The father of the classic financial con." Again he raised his glass in tribute, and took another swallow.

Hannibal lowered his voice and leaned closer. "This is your thing, isn't it? Was that Weston-Wellesley Investment Services?"

"A focused investment firm," Monroe said, swirling his drink. "We specialized in purchasing small firms in the transportation, trash, courier and fuel oil industries. Nicely diversified, don't you think?"

"Just what the beginning investor wants to hear," Hannibal said. "But in fact, just a multimillion-dollar pyramid scheme that offered exorbitant returns but long term just pumped money into your pocket."

"Look, my regular investment work did real well," Monroe said, his words slurring just enough for Hannibal to notice. "But when the market moved against us, we knew how to keep the investors happy. The way we combined the standard pyramid scheme with Ponzi was an inspired innovation. So whenever things got too slow, or I had a liquidity problem, well, I'd just fire up a company like Weston-Wellesley Investments for a while."

"So this is how you took Cindy Santiago's money. And Jason Moore's. And whoever else threw big money at you?" Hannibal had to raise his voice just a little over two men arguing at the bar.

"Well, it might surprise you to know that I don't even recognize those names, so they didn't invest what I consider big money. Now real estate mogul John Leotta, that guy was a whale. In fact he single handedly funded a whole wave of dividends. It was his money that drew in that last crop of young lawyers."

"Really? Cindy was just one of a basket full of young lawyers you suckered?"

Monroe stared at him with lowered brows, as if he hadn't heard at first. Then his mouth dropped open and he nodded. "I see. This Cindy, this is your woman, isn't it?" he said, grinning and winking. "I took your woman, and maybe a close friend. Sure. That's why you're involved. You don't give a damn about Irene."

A blinding flash of rage locked Hannibal's jaws making him speechless for a moment. It would be so easy to knock a few of this drunken swindler's teeth down his throat, but that would serve no purpose. Hannibal did have a few choice words for Wash, once he got his anger back under control.

Before Hannibal could put his thoughts into words a loud thump behind him drew his attention. He turned to see one husky fellow in a plaid shirt and jeans had slammed another into the bar. If this place had a bouncer, he needed to evict those two before it got ugly.

"You're wrong, Wash. I didn't know her, but I sure as hell care. I care that some asshole gunned her down right in front of me, like me being a witness didn't matter. And I care because I think she was a nice woman trying to do the right thing for two people you screwed over. But they weren't the only two. You might not have hurt Irene, but I'm betting this is why you sent the Larsons away. They knew too much and you were afraid they might talk. And now, you got nobody."

Out the corner of his eye Hannibal saw that a third man had joined in with the two at the bar. Instead of calming them down he seemed to be making it worse. Others were starting to egg them on, pushing for a fight to relieve their own boredom.

"Hey, you can't be too sure about that stuff." Monroe said, getting louder over the general babble in the room. "I was pretty wild in my younger days. For all you know I got a little bastard out there looking for me."

Hannibal was only half listening to Monroe, his eyes on the growing turmoil at the bar. All eyes were on the three men now wrestling around, still on foot but sure to hit the floor soon. The bartender was shouting now, and pulled out a small bat with which he presumably intended to reduce the number of troublemakers. And in the midst of the loud voices he heard glass breaking.

Hannibal spun to look at Monroe. Like everyone else in the room, Monroe's eyes were on the fight at the bar. Well, almost everyone else. The black man coming up behind Monroe looked Hannibal right in the eye. He wore a gray George Mason University sweatshirt with the hood up, shadowing his face. His right hand held the neck of a broken bottle. He swung the green glass weapon up in a wide arc toward Monroe's neck.

There was no time to be gentle.

Hannibal swung his right palm in a quick backhand, slapping Monroe's head out of the way. Then his left hand snapped out, capturing the wrist behind the bottle. He spun as he stood, turning his back to the attacker and locking the captured arm under his left armpit. Leaning hard, he slammed the attacker's face down on the table. Then he just had to give the man's pinky a good yank to make him drop the bottle.

"What the hell?" Monroe said, pulling himself up from the floor by leaning on the edge of the table. His voice was just one more distraction before one of the bruisers shoved another, who slammed into someone else, who crashed down on Hannibal's table. The table flipped. Hannibal swung his right arm around to break his fall as he hit the floor. His wrist thumped the edge of a neighboring table, sending a nasty jolt of pain up his arm. A woman, thrown off balance, crashed down on him, her behind shoving the breath out of his stomach. He shoved her away, only regretting his roughness for a second. He had to get to his feet.

Then a nightstick slammed down on a table and a coarse voice bellowed, "All right, let's have some order here."

The two uniformed policemen at the door looked across the roomful of men and women like stern parents and for their part the tavern's residents looked suitably embarrassed. Hannibal figured the bartender probably called for them at the first sign of trouble. He scanned the bar quickly but didn't see the gray hoodie. Monroe's attacker must have made it out the door in the confusion. Hannibal charged for the entrance, shoving two men out of his way. Two steps later a palm shoved into his chest stopped his forward momentum.

"What's your hurry, sir?" the cop asked, somehow making the word "sir" sound just like "boy."

"Officer, a guy just tried to kill my friend and if we move fast enough we might catch him." Hannibal tried to force his way past the two cops but one used his nightstick to shove him back.

"Yeah, I know we missed a couple of the guys that were here, but we'll want to question the rest and that includes you."

Hannibal cursed silently and backed off, showing his palms. He figured he wanted these guys to see him as the cooperative sort. That was the image he wanted them to have if they decided to start frisking people and found the automatic under his left arm. But as he backed up Monroe stepped forward, standing too straight the way drunks so often do.

"Gentlemen I am George Washington Monroe and this fellow is in my employ. I can vouch for him. We have been working with inspector Orson Rissik."

"Well if you'll have a seat there, Mr. Monroe, we'll see if we can contact Detective Rissik for you."

## -12-

Hannibal wondered if Rissik ever looked tired. Sitting in his little office at the Fairfax County complex, his suit coat on a hanger on the back of the door and his sleeves rolled up in neat folds, he looked as if he was just about to get down to the real work of the day.

Hannibal liked visiting Rissik's office because he liked order. He got comfortable in his usual visitor's chair. Monroe walked the office as if making it his own, stopping to read the three framed citations hanging on the wall and stare for a moment at the poster hanging behind the desk. On it, a pelican held a frog in its mouth, but the frog had reached out and wrapped a hand around the pelican's throat, preventing it from swallowing him. Monroe tapped the caption and nodded.

"Never give up, eh? I have a feeling that many a felon has regretted getting your attention."

Rissik waited for Monroe to limp to a chair and settle in before answering. "Yeah, well some guys think they're untouchable. I like to prove them wrong. Now, since you're sitting here in my office I guess I need to get a statement from you guys. What the hell happened in that bar?"

"Honestly, officer, I don't really know very much," Monroe said, straightening his tie. "We were having a quiet bite to eat and a few drinks and a fight broke out. Then I seem to have fallen off my chair."

Rissik had stopped listening six words into Monroe's comments and turned his eyes to Hannibal. Hannibal glanced at the table on the other side of the office.

"I don't think the fight just broke out, Chief, but you know I think better with coffee. I can't believe your coffee pot over there is empty."

"Yeah, I cut it off at six every day, so I might be able to sleep if I decide to go home. But don't worry, I sent Gert out for Starbucks just before you got here."

"Gert's still at work?"

"Yeah, she tends to stay as long as I'm here. I don't ask. She just stays."

"Uh-huh." Hannibal shook his head. "Well, while we're waiting, might as well tell you what I saw. Three guys started a commotion over by the bar, but it wasn't serious. I don't think a punch was ever thrown. They were just a distraction."

"Really?" Rissik leaned forward, resting his elbows on his desk. "Distraction for who? Or from what?"

As Hannibal opened his mouth to speak a solidly-built brunette who could have been twenty-eight or fifty-eight years old marched into the room. She wore a conservative navy business suit, with a skirt long enough to prevent anyone knowing whether or not her legs were worth staring at. She offered Hannibal a large coffee, then handed a cup to Monroe and placed a third on Rissik's desk.

"Cream? Sugar?" she asked. When Monroe nodded she retrieved his coffee and took it to the side table. While he talked her through the preparations, Hannibal continued.

"For the entire bar full of random people. From the little guy with the broken bottle. It didn't feel like a random attack to me, but it would have looked like one if I hadn't been sitting there."

Monroe's head whipped around. "You think that man there specifically to hurt me?"

"Wash, that guy was too far away from the fight to want to knock the end off a beer bottle," Hannibal said. "He wasn't headed for the bar. He was headed for your neck. And under normal circumstances, he'd have opened your neck with that bottle and been gone in the confusion before anybody even knew what happened."

"You can't know that," Monroe said.

"Yeah, who'd want to hurt a sweet guy like you?" Rissik asked.

"Snark does not become you, officer."

"Detective."

"Whatever."

"So how about I just get a written statement from each of you and then you can go home where there probably isn't anybody who wants to kill you."

"Where there isn't anybody," Monroe said. "I release the help on weekends."

Ignoring Monroe's bitter tone, Hannibal waved a dismissive hand at Rissik. "There's nobody to press charges against, and the victim obviously doesn't care. Do you want to get out of here and get statements in the morning? What are you doing here this late anyway?"

"Ahh, you know how much paperwork and BS is involved when you find a body." When he saw the puzzled expression on Hannibal's face, he said, "Didn't you know? We found him." Rissik stopped short, pointing toward Monroe as if he was a reason to stop talking. Hannibal swatted the notion away with his hand.

"You mean Jason? You found Jason Moore? Where?"

"Who?" Monroe asked.

"The boyfriend," Hannibal said without looking at him. "You thought he ran off with your wife. Instead somebody killed him to sell the runaway story. What did they do to him, Chief?"

"Actually I kind of thought I'd like to get your gut level impressions of all that," Rissik said, leaning forward on his elbows. "Besides, you know we can't make it official based on a photo. We need a personal identification. You want to see the body?"

"Hey I would like a chance to examine him. But, I do have an errand I need to run first."

Monroe looked lost when Hannibal pulled up in front of his house. He stared up at the front door of his colonial palace. A row of lights along the drive and two more in the portico ceiling made the flight of stairs leading up to the door as bright as day. Hannibal wondered if he feared the darkness beyond the door.

"Want to come in for a drink?" Monroe asked, but his voice revealed that he already knew the answer.

"You'll be fine, Wash," Hannibal said. "And the last thing you need right now is a drink. Just go on in, and make sure you reset the alarm when you get inside."

"It's a big enough pain in the ass getting in," Monroe said. "Now you want me to lock myself in?"

"Well, I don't think anybody would go in there looking for you," Hannibal said. "That's not this guy's M.O. But no sense taking stupid chances. Besides, I imagine you'll sleep pretty soundly tonight."

"Yeah, probably. You know, um...I'm sorry."

"What about?"

Monroe kept his eyes on the dashboard. "I'm sorry your woman lost her money. And I'm sorry this guy Jason Moore is dead, especially if he died just to cover up Irene's murder. I know it doesn't make anything any better. I just wanted to say I'm sorry."

A little short of an admission of guilt, Hannibal thought, but a bigger step than he expected. He looked at Monroe as if seeing him for the first time. "You're not quite who I thought you were, Wash."

Monroe smirked. "Me too."

"I think maybe your hero Ponzi was able to do what he did because he never let himself consider that the people he took were live human beings just trying to make it in this world, like him. Maybe he never had to see the consequences of his work."

"Yeah, maybe," Monroe said. "Or maybe he was just having too much fun proving he was smarter than everybody else."

"Look, you go on inside and get some sleep, Wash. I got detective work to do if I'm going to find the people who took Irene away from you."

Monroe nodded and left the car without saying goodnight. Hannibal thought the shrubs and bushes were too close to the door, so he sat and watched Monroe climb the outside stairs. He watched him fumble with his keys. He stayed until Monroe was inside. He watched lights come on and move upstairs. Then, on an impulse he got out of his car, walked to the door and tried the knob. He felt better knowing for sure that the door was locked.

Back in his car he opened the vents and let the cool air blow in his face. That kept him alert on the drive back to Fairfax. It was nearly an hour round trip. He knew any sane cop would have told him to forget coming back to the Braddock Road complex that night. He also knew that when he parked on the other side of police headquarters, walked into the medical examiner's office and continued down the hall to the morgue, Orson Rissik would still be sitting there, looking around as if he couldn't figure out why everybody else was gone for the day.

The state medical examiner's mortuary was not the dark, atmospheric cavern you see in old movies. Nor was it the cold, antiseptic space so often portrayed on television. Instead, it was exactly what it should have been, a medical examination room. This, Hannibal thought, was where the real forensic work was done, where experts measured core temperatures, judged lividity, checked the progress of rigor mortis, looked for insect larvae and determined when and how the most recent corpse came to be their guest. In every way it was like any other laboratory in any hospital. Hannibal didn't mind the brightness, but he could never get used to the antiseptic smell.

Rissik greeted him with a nod and walked him through the high-ceilinged rooms, their steps echoing on the tile floors. They were in the room lined with stainless steel drawers before either of them felt the need to speak.

"Hey, am I supposed to be in here?"

"You are as far as Billy is concerned," Rissik said. "I told him you were a relative of the deceased, come for the ID." Then he called out to Billy, the long-haired, pimple-faced lab tech who was stuck with night duty. He strolled in, tossed off hellos and walked to a particular drawer. He grabbed the handle and looked up at Hannibal.

"Are you ready for this?"

"I'll be strong," Hannibal said. It wasn't his first dead body after all.

Billy nodded solemnly and pulled the handle. The drawer slid forward on silent rollers. Billy stepped back and Hannibal found himself face-to-face with Jason Moore. He had seen a few corpses and it always gave him an initial shiver that people looked so much like nothing had changed after life had left them. Jason was a little paler than Hannibal remembered but otherwise very much himself. He took a deep breath and reminded himself that this was not the man he met three days ago, but just the shell he used to live in.

"Jason Moore?" Rissik asked.

"Jason Moore. This is what you wanted me to see. This does not look like a man who's been dead for three days."

"No, he is pretty well preserved."

"So where'd you find him," Hannibal asked, "and what was the cause of death?"

Rissik crossed his arms and leaned against the drawers. "Well as you can see, there's been no autopsy yet. They brought him in after four so the medical examiner will get to him tomorrow. But I don't need an official pronouncement to guess. Check his neck."

Hannibal slipped a gloved hand under the dead man's head and probed the vertebrae. He stopped at number six. His stomach clenched but nothing showed on his face. It isn't Jason, he told himself again.

"Yeah, it's broken."

"Yeah, but how?" Rissik asked. "I know they gave you some forensic training in New York and probably more at Treasury."

"The Secret Service doesn't do that kind of stuff," Hannibal said. "But they did in New York City detective school. Besides, I've felt this before."

"So? Blunt force trauma? Or did they toss him down the stairs?"

"No, this is radial trauma," Hannibal said.

"What?"

Hannibal closed his eyes but didn't move his hand. "Somebody stood behind this man, grabbed his head and gave it a sharp twist, snapping his neck. Quick. Merciful I guess."

"And cold blooded," Rissik said. "These people are icicles."

"At least one of them is a trained killer," Hannibal said. "The shooter was very calm and clean. But that doesn't account for the body being so fresh."

"When we searched his house we found the body downstairs. How many single guys have a chest freezer? Naturally we had to look inside. Turns out it was pretty convenient for the killers that he had one."

"Not the brightest place to leave the body," Hannibal said, very slowly sliding his hand out from under Jason's neck.

"I don't know about that," Rissik said. "If we found him weeks later, placing time of death would have been pretty near impossible. And not hauling him out of the house was a pretty smart play, or would have been if not for you. Absent your insistence that Irene Monroe was murdered, everyone would be looking for both of them in Canada. If we believed he ran off we never would have searched his house."

Hannibal nodded, looked down at Jason for another second, and slowly slid his drawer closed. "Cold and calculating. Damn, I hope the same guy who shot Irene Monroe did this. I don't want to find out there are two or three killers this smart and deadly out there, but it sure could be a cell."

"Yeah, that's why I didn't want to wait for the autopsy."

"Wait a sec," Hannibal spun to face Rissik. "No autopsy, but you said you found him around four. You found him while I was running around with Wash?" When Rissik nodded, he asked, "Why the hell didn't you call me right away?"

Rissik shrugged. "I didn't think I'd need to. Kind of surprised Santiago didn't tell you."

Hannibal lost a beat as his world collapsed in on itself and then exploded back out. In that instant he felt every second that had passed since the last time he spoke to his woman.

"You told Cindy? You told her you found Jason's body?"

Rissik took a step back, palms up in mock defense. "Hey, she called looking for you. I guess she thought you were with me. Anyway, she asked if there was any news, and I knew he was her friend so yeah. I guess I just assumed she'd call you next. You haven't heard from her?"

Rissik said more but Hannibal didn't hear it. He was already running for the door, plotting the fastest way to his hotel room.

A coworker in his secret service days once remarked that Hannibal Jones was "wired wrong." When a man stuck a gun in his face, his reaction was more anger than fear. His fellow agent jumped to the conclusion that Hannibal was immune to fear.

He was wrong. At that moment, fumbling with his plastic card room key, Hannibal was terrified. His imagination raked him with thoughts of what Cindy might do faced with confirmation of her friend's death. Her mental state seemed so fragile when he left that day. Why in God's name had he not called to check on her throughout the day? Was he so obsessed with observing Wash, with what was happening in the moment? Or was he just so accustomed to Cindy being able to handle anything that he put her out of his mind while he was gone? No matter what, he spent the entire drive beating himself up for inexcusable self-centered bad judgement.

Once he got the door unlocked he shoved it open as if he expected an ambush. The room was dark except for the moon glow coming through the windows. It was soft indirect lighting like the kind you see in a movie that you're supposed to interpret as total darkness. He wanted to see her sleeping form lying in the bed, but it was not there. He turned toward the windows and that was when fear wrapped its icy fingers around his heart and squeezed.

He took it in all at once without any processing time. Cindy sat slouched in the chair over by the window as still as a corpse, wearing only her lacy silk black bra and panties. She was backlit just as he had been that morning, except that the sunlight had given her skin a golden glow while the moonlight stole the color from her flesh. One small foot was curled under her while the other dangled toward the floor. He head lolled back and to her left. Her hands rested on the tables to either side of the chair.

The Unisom pack lay beside her left hand. The flat plastic and foil pill card was pushed out of its colorful sleeve. The fingers of her right hand were curled up against a light rum bottle as if she had been holding the bottle and then her hand had simply fallen from it. The bottle was three-quarters empty.

Arms spread, head tilted, one leg bent, she looked like some sick take on a crucifix with the pills on one side and the rum bottle on the other serving as the nails holding her hands in place.

Hannibal's chest imploded, forcing a hoarse, guttural sound out of him. It was somehow less than a scream but more than a crying sob.

## -13-

Hannibal forced himself to breathe and rushed toward Cindy. But after three steps he pulled up short when her head snapped up and her eyes popped open.

Fear contorted her features and her mouth gaped wide, pushing out an inarticulate scream. Hannibal stopped and even took a small step backward when he realized that it was his form speeding toward her that had frightened her.

"What? What?" Cindy stared left and right, eyes wide, panting hard.

"Easy, babe," Hannibal said, palms forward. "You scared the shit out of me. Are you all right?"

"I scared you?" Cindy leaned forward as if to stand. Her eyes rolled upward and she slumped back down into the chair. Hannibal started forward but her raised hand stopped him. Then she looked again left and right, took in the objects that she must have been holding when she passed out and raised her eyebrows.

"Oh. I see." She raised a small half-smile and picked up the rum bottle as if to see how much she drank. Hannibal watched her closely, her soft golden face and shoulders caressed by the moonlight. He watched thoughts dance across her face but had no idea how to react to what he saw.

"Nothing to say?" Cindy asked, her words just a little slurred. "It's okay. I get it. When you came in I was passed out. You saw the pills and the booze and you figured I couldn't stand to accept that some little shit killed Jason. Right? You thought I curled up in this chair and committed suicide."

When he opened his mouth to speak, she thrust her right palm at him to freeze the words in his throat. Then she picked up the little packet of pills and began to turn it in her hand, examining it as if it were some ancient artifact no one had ever seen before. Then she smiled. Not at Hannibal, but at the pills.

"I could have done it, you know. I thought about it. I was here all alone and I thought about it. I couldn't talk to you. I couldn't even talk to Daddy. It would have meant admitting failure that I had given up. I didn't want to figure out what to do next, how to start over. I just wanted to go to sleep and forget the losses. And I had these little beauties."

She turned to face Hannibal. "Diphenhydro...dyphun... hmmm...I guess I did drink a bit." She shook her head and focused on the package in her hand. "Diphenhydramine. That's what's in these things. Kind of a mild sedative. Each one is 50 milligrams. Anything over 300 milligrams is considered an overdose. So, with 18 of these and a nice bottle of rum I could have just gone away. No pain, no anger, no guilt, no shame, no embarrassment, just a nap that would never end. I really thought about it. I could have done it so easily."

"Yeah, but you didn't," Hannibal said, sitting on the edge of the bed.

"Nope. I just doubled the dosage on the rum side." She picked up the bottle by its neck and sloshed its contents around. "I looked myself in the face and decided that I wasn't going to do it. I could have, I just wouldn't. Know why?"

He did, but he shook his head. He knew she needed to say it.

"Because," she said, leaning forward, "It would have meant admitting failure. That I had given up."

Hannibal's heart swelled then and he stood up and gathered his woman into his arms. She stood to embrace him and he could almost feel the last of the fear and uncertainty seep out of her.

"I love you," he whispered.

"Do you?" When he nodded, she asked, "Will you forgive me for being a baby and blaming you, God and everybody else for my bad time?"

"Nothing to forgive."

After three deep, shaky breaths she asked, "Will you find the bastard who killed my friend?"

"I promise," He said, noting with a smile that she made no mention of the lost money.

She hugged him tighter. "Will you take me to bed and make me forget who I've been for the last couple of days?"

Hannibal lifted, and Cindy slipped her legs up and around his waist. He turned and walked toward the bed.

"Welcome back, babe."

She awakened him by nipping at his chest with her tiny, perfect teeth. The sun, just crawling over the horizon, burst through the window and made the room so bright it blinded him. Hannibal took the two hints and rolled over onto her. His mouth covered hers and she moaned low and opened herself completely to him.

The night before their lovemaking had been fast and hard. Hannibal made their morning love agonizingly slow, but no less intense. Cindy strung her releases together like pearls on a necklace, each a tiny bit bigger than the last until he couldn't stand the pressure any longer and added his voice to hers.

Later, when Hannibal was propped up on two pillows sipping room service coffee, Cindy was still wearing her mischievous grin. "You really like that don't you Poppy?"

"What?"

"You know," she said, lightly punching him in the ribs. "That part when you give me a temporary case of Tourette's syndrome."

"Well, yeah. You never use that kind of language any other time, do you? And I love it when you start throwing Spanish at me, even though I don't understand a word of it."

"Maybe not, honey, but you always seem to get the right message."

They decided to take advantage of it being Sunday and enjoy a leisurely brunch. They lazed in the room until after ten o'clock, watching music television and cuddling without much conversation. When they finally got up Cindy took Hannibal's hand and led him to the bathroom. There they shared a hot shower, lathering each other and scrubbing each other's back. Playful teasing pushed business further and further from their minds.

Back in the bedroom Cindy pulled on a casual blouse and a skirt that was a couple of inches shorter than her usual business wear. Swayed by the view of her perfect legs Hannibal grudgingly agreed to leave his gloves and tie in the room, and to park his sunglasses in an inside suit jacket pocket.

The dining room glowed with the golden sunlight and the couple enjoyed the muted atmosphere. Hannibal ordered steak and eggs, while Cindy went for something more exotic.

"Fish for breakfast?" Hannibal asked when their orders arrived. The aroma might have been pleasant if it didn't clash so hard with the steak.

"You are a heathen," Cindy said, picking up her fork. "First of all, this is brunch, not breakfast. And this lovely orange sesame glazed smoked salmon is insulted to be referred to simply as fish."

"Right. Fish with an attitude." Hannibal sliced into his own food, noting the perfect pink inside the steak and swirling it in an egg yolk.

"Well you certainly made good on your commitment last night, kind sir," Cindy said with a wink.

"One does what one can. And I had some excellent inspiration."

Cindy looked down and focused on her plate. "So, what about your other promise last night? Are you going to find Jason's killer?"

Hannibal sighed around a mouthful of meat. The steak was perfectly crunchy on the outside and moist on the inside. Why was she in such a hurry to spoil their meal with business?

"Yes, dear, I will find him."

"And will you take him out?"

Hannibal eyes went to the ceiling before finding Cindy again and he pushed back from the table a bit, hands spread wide. "What, you want me to put a bullet in his dome? I've got one suspect who might have enough of a motive and I'm going to try to get a read on him when I leave here. But even if it turns out to be him I don't think I'm ready to carry out any frontier justice. What I will do is make sure he faces justice. With two premeditated murders and another failed attempt, there's no doubt a Virginia jury will give him the death penalty."

"Good," she said in a calm voice that Hannibal found a bit unsettling. "And what about George Monroe?"

"Wash? What about him?" Hannibal began the efficient process of policing up all of the egg yolk with a piece of toast.

"Is he the man who swindled Jason and me out of our savings?"

The question was too direct to dodge. "I don't have any hard evidence but yes, I believe he is. He's also the man who lost his wife a few days ago. And I'll be getting together with him later today to try to follow the trail to the killer, or killers."

"Really?" Cindy took small, ladylike bites of the salmon. "What do you think he can tell you?"

"He's my best shot at pinning down everybody who might have motive," Hannibal said.

Cindy started a sentence with, "Well, I'm..." changed it to, "I want to," and finally settled on, "May I come with you?" Her head was still down but she looked up from under her brows at him.

Hannibal smiled and nodded, again thinking to himself, "Welcome back, babe."

They took a short, quiet drive to meet Hannibal's next suspect. Cindy's hand settled onto his thigh but she stared out the windshield. Hannibal knew she had something on her mind, but it would be up to her to open the conversation. When they pulled up to the security gate He gave his name to the elderly uniformed guard and had his ID ready, but it was unnecessary.

"No problem, sir," said the guard, staring through thick reading glasses. "You're right here on Mr. Leotta's guest list.

Couldn't miss a name like yours. Go straight up and then right to the clubhouse parking."

"So how did you know to bring us here?" Cindy asked as Hannibal pulled into the parking lot.

"A couple of phone calls was all it took," he said, slipping into a space between a Lexus and Jaguar. "And no surprise. Where else would you find a real estate mover and shaker on a Sunday morning? Talking business during church is still frowned upon."

On his way to opening Cindy's door, Hannibal let his eyes wander across the grounds of the River Bend Golf and Country Club. As a non-player all such clubs looked the same to him. The gently rolling countryside yielded such an open view in all directions it gave the impression of being miles from any civilization. The well treed and carefully manicured grounds were primed for promotional photos. The air was crisp and sweet. Even the birds contributed to the pastoral scene, warbling as if auditioning for a Disney cartoon.

"Don't you play?" Cindy asked as they walked under the brick arch in front of the clubhouse. "I've never seen you but I always assumed…"

"Never not once," Hannibal replied. "Just can't see spoiling a long walk through the woods by batting a tiny white ball around." As close as they were, it was funny what they didn't know about each other. Inside the clubhouse was all leather and hardwood, the atmosphere jovial but subdued. Cindy wore her cocktail hour smile but Hannibal's senses went on alert. He had scanned the room and noted only one other person of color. That man moved toward Hannibal as soon as they made eye contact. He was much darker than Hannibal and had him by two inches of height and a good forty pounds. And while Hannibal kept his expression neutral the other man's face was hard. Not street thug hard but rather Marine Corps or Ranger hard.

Hannibal moved his right foot back and his hands just below his waist. This subtle ready stance would mean nothing to a casual observer but the man moving toward him nodded and stopped outside of arm's reach.

"Mr. Leotta will meet you in the upstairs lounge."

The other man turned and walked toward a flight of stairs. Hannibal took Cindy's hand and followed. Halfway up the stairs he spoke to the back of the other man's head.

"You know who I am, right? Hannibal Jones. Private investigator."

"Cramer," the other man replied without turning around.

Hannibal had not seen recognition in Cramer's eyes but did consider that he was big enough to be the man in the bar with the broken bottle. If it came to a conflict, he would be a hard man to put down.

Cramer held the door for Hannibal and Cindy to enter, then followed them in and stood by the door. The lounge was paneled in the kind of dark wood that makes you imagine you smell cigar smoke. Four overstuffed leather chairs stood at the corners of a large oak table. Two of the chairs were occupied by athletic blonds wearing white golf shirts and brown loafers. The woman wore a knee length shirt and sat back in her chair with her ankles crossed. The man, in khakis, sat forward on the balls of his feet. As Cramer closed the door he stood and stretched a hand toward Hannibal.

"John Leotta. This is my wife Joan."

After freeing himself from Leotta's fierce handshake Hannibal shook Joan's hand more gently and introduced Cindy. She and Hannibal settled into their chairs. John Leotta returned to his perch at the edge of his leather cushion.

"You said you had questions about investing with Weston-Wellesley?" Straight to the point. This guy just bled nervous energy. He was like a puppy having trouble sitting still, and his biceps told Hannibal that he burned off a lot of that energy in the gym. His wife, on the other hand, was a portrait of calm confidence. They would be a good team.

"Yes, and I hope I didn't give you cause for concern," Hannibal said. "I'm only here to talk today."

Leotta turned his head to the side the way a dog does, with a look of confusion. "Why would you say such a thing?"

Hannibal cast an eye toward the door. "Cramer here is not your personal assistant."

"No, Cramer is security. He's not here because of you, he's here to watch over Joan."

"You're concerned for her safety?" Cindy asked.

"Yes. That's in connection with Weston-Wellesley investments too."

Hannibal leaned forward and lowered his voice. "Mr. Leotta I really need to discuss some financial details with you. Perhaps we should excuse ourselves and leave the ladies to…"

"Nono," Leotta said, waving the notion away. "We discuss this together. I have no secrets from my wife."

Hannibal had heard that from any number of husbands, and wondered if it was ever true. In this case, he would proceed as if it was the truth.

"John, you should know that I'm here because of George Washington Monroe. He told me that you and he have done business."

"Did he?" Leotta asked. "Did he? I see. You and your lawyer here, you're trying to tie me in to Wash's crooked business, is that it?"

Cindy spoke up. "Mr. Leotta I don't think we're…"

"That son of a bitch," Leotta said. "Did he tell you how he came in here, to this club, cozying up to the most successful guys? Did he tell you that after I sold him that house he offered me a special opportunity? Did he tell you how I eventually sank more than 800,000 dollars into Weston-Wellesley investments? Yeah, that's how much of my money vanished when the company went under. What else did you want to know?"

Cindy started to speak again, but Hannibal waved her to silence. "That sounds like a pretty good reason to be angry."

"You bet I'm pissed. I'm not in with that crook."

"Angry enough to want to hurt him, I think," Hannibal said, glancing back at Cramer. "Mr. Monroe was attacked recently."

"What? So I'm a suspect now?" Leotta bounced to his feet. Hannibal matched his action so they stood face to face. He felt Cramer step closer behind him.

From deep in her chair, Joan Leotta said, "If you think that, you don't know my husband at all. That's not his style. He's suing Monroe of course. But nothing primitive. Besides, Monroe has more important things on his mind."

"You are referring to the rumor that his wife has run off with a younger man?" Cindy asked.

"Boy, you guys are out of it," Leotta said. He sat, Hannibal followed suit, and Cramer returned to his post at the door. "I know that's the official story. But…" Leotta slid forward to the edge of his chair and leaned in as if some outsider might be listening. In a low tone he said, "My insider with the Fairfax County police tells me the truth is, she was abducted and murdered. I figure whoever had it in for Wash went after his wife instead."

Hannibal and Cindy exchanged a glance. With a serious expression, Cindy said, "You think Mrs. Monroe met with foul play?"

"Why do you think we have Cramer here? I figured if Wash had that kind of enemies it had to have something to do with his investment firm. Whoever he pissed off could just as soon go after anybody he was in business with. And even though I lost a bundle, all anybody really knows is that I sank a boatload of dollars into Wash's enterprises. That's kind of public knowledge around here."

"So to be safe you hired a bodyguard," Hannibal said.

"Yep. Called him in yesterday morning first thing when I got the word about Wash's wife."

"You mean he watched you, and Joan, all day?" Hannibal asked.

"Look at my wife, Mr. Jones. You think I want to risk losing this?" He turned a puppy-dog smile on her, then turned back to Hannibal. "Home and away, until I'm sure the threat is over. Last night he kept an eye on us at Morton's when we went to dinner. We met friends at the bar in the Hyatt and stayed out pretty late actually, but I felt safe as long as I could put eyes on Cramer, and he could see us."

"Yes, I'm sure he provides a feeling of security."

Leotta leaned back with arms folded, looking smug the way some people do when they're sure they know something you don't. "So, Mr. Jones, what else did you want to ask me? Or accuse me of?"

"I think that will do it for now," Hannibal said, standing. "I appreciate your openness, and I'll contact you if we need anything else."

Hannibal took Cindy's hand to help her to her feet. The Leottas also stood, and Joan asked, "The police will find the people who did this, won't they?"

"They will, or I will," Hannibal said.

"It is terrible whatever happened to Mrs. Monroe of course but, well, do you think these people will hurt anyone else?"

Cindy clenched her eyes tight and looked down and away. Only Hannibal saw the pain on her face. He saw no point in sharing any more detail with the Leottas, so he kept his answer to, "We'll do everything we can to get to the bottom of this."

On the way to the car Hannibal wondered if walking through eighteen holes of well-tended woods would relax the kind of tensions he deals with on a daily basis. When he had the engine purring he told Cindy, "We've got one more stop."

"You don't think Leotta has anything to do with what happened to Irene Monroe and Jason, do you?"

"Doesn't seem likely," Hannibal said. "I can see why Wash might have picked him out of the crowd here. Leotta may as well have 'mark' written on his forehead. No grafter could resist taking advantage of him. But I'm thinking Wash is starting to regret taking advantage of so many people to climb to the top of his personal mountain. He was kind of weird when I dropped him off."

Once they were on the road they lapsed into silence. Even through Hannibal's Oakleys, the sun gave the world around him a surreal brightness. He flipped the CD player to the energetic jazz of the Crusaders and pushed his car to just a few miles per hour over the speed limit. Cindy leaned against the passenger door and turned so that her left knee pressed against Hannibal's thigh.

"So tell me about him. Who is George Washington Monroe?"

"Wash?" Hannibal mulled the question for a moment. "Well, he's black. He's handsome. He's as smooth as any con man I've ever met, but downright charming, even when he isn't running a game."

"Or at least, when you don't think he's running a game." Cindy said with a wink.

"Okay, counselor, fair enough. If he's as good as I think he is, I wouldn't know when he was scamming me. But I'm absolutely convinced of one thing. The man loved his wife."

When the car phone buzzed it startled them both. Cindy had never heard it before. Hannibal had only given the number to a few people and she was the most frequent user. He didn't figure it could be good news, but it was probably news he wanted. He tapped the button on his steering wheel to answer the call and turn on the speakers.

"This is Hannibal."

"Hey, Jones, it's Orson." The voice filled the car. "I see I caught you in the car so you're headed somewhere, but I think you'll want to postpone that appointment."

"No emergency," Hannibal said. "Where are you? And what are you doing calling me on a Sunday? Don't you ever take a day off?"

"Crime don't take the weekends off," Rissik said. "I'm at Monroe's place, and I think you ought to get out here too."

"You're in luck, buddy," Hannibal said. "I'm five minutes away."

The remainder of the drive was a blur for Hannibal. With almost no traffic resistance he was able to push the Volvo to its limits on mostly straight, well-paved roads. Even in Northern Virginia, they were far enough south that autumn looked a lot like spring. Most of the trees never fully shed their leaves and the evergreens filled in the spaces. Snow almost never covered the ground and grass just turned from a bright green to a duller shade of the same color. But the world did smell different, and as he approached Monroe's home the odor took a definite sharp turn. The comforting scent he associated with fireplaces proved grating that day.

Hannibal pulled into the circular driveway and stepped out of his car without a word. He stared over the vehicle's roof at the broad swath of smoking timbers and ash where the palatial colonial home was the day before. The pile of rubble hardly seemed big enough to represent the house it had replaced, and shrubs and bushes that stood too close to the house had paid the price.

## -14-

"Last night, or rather this morning, apparently just before dawn." Rissik kept his voice low, as if they were already at the funeral. He seemed dressed for one too, in a navy blue suit, starched dress shirt and tie. He stood just behind Hannibal and to one side with his hands in his pockets. Cindy walked around the car to stand beside Hannibal. She slid her hand into his and followed his gaze to the smoking rubble.

He watched two investigators picking through the debris. The sun warmed his exposed skin and he imagined that it was from the fire that had raged through the house just hours before. "Wash was inside?" he asked in the same muted tone Rissik had used.

"In bed," Rissik said. "Smoking a cigar, according to the examiners. And with the remains of three bottles on the bed, one could assume that two were empty."

"Hard to believe this could even happen," Hannibal said. "I know the house had a sprinkler system. The construction on places like these is amazing. And these days, firefighter response times are so impressive."

"Yeah, but before they can scramble somebody has to notice the fire and then call it in. Look around you. Imagine how big the blaze would have had to be before any of the neighbors could even see it. The firemen fought this one hard but as I understand it, the house was fully engulfed by the time they got the word."

Cindy continued to stare straight ahead. "You can't think this was an accident."

"Despite what you may have heard, Miss Santiago," Rissik said, "Becoming a police detective doesn't make you stupid. Still, an objective eye or a defense attorney could make a credible case for suicide. Expensive booze aside, there is no evidence of an accelerant. The condition of the body will make it impossible for anyone to know just how drunk he was when the fire started."

Cindy swallowed. "Point taken. You mentioned the body. He's not still in there, is he?"

Rissik smiled. "Taken away hours before the local cops thought to let me know about the fire, ma'am. But I understand there wasn't much to examine."

"Thanks for your patience. And please call me Cindy. Once we've taken a meal together…"

Hannibal interrupted. "Got a cause of death?"

"They're thinking smoke inhalation," Rissik said. "But the medical examiner isn't completely sure he can tie all of the damage to the body to the falling debris. For example, there is the matter of the seventh vertebrae."

Hannibal tried to picture Monroe, drunk in his bed and surrounded by partially empty bottles. He passes out late in the night. Alcohol spills onto the covers. A lit cigar drops from his mouth. Flames spread quickly through the room. Death from smoke inhalation. Minutes later, before the fire department arrives, a heavy timber drops from above crashing into his head and breaking his neck.

Possible. Plausible. But the human hands of a trained killer seemed somehow easier for him to believe. If someone could get into the house. But the alarm was set. Who would Wash have invited in? He was lost in thought until he felt his hand being squeezed.

"Hannibal? Is there a reason we need to keep standing here?"

The breeze shifted, forcing the smoke from the smoldering mass to follow them as they walked down the driveway toward the street. The smoke wasn't thick, or even visible, but it filled Hannibal's lungs like a thick cloud of guilt.

"Right out from under me," he muttered. "Again."

"Don't you even start that shit," Rissik said. "He didn't get the message in that bar, did he? How many times can you save a man's life in 24 hours?"

"It's the same guy, isn't it?" Cindy asked. "I mean, it has to be, right?"

"Sure seems that way," Rissik said. "Which I guess takes Monroe out of the suspect pool for his wife's death." A green Jaguar slowed to a crawl as it passed in front of the house. Rissik held up his badge and waved the car on. "Damn rubberneckers. So what do you think of Leotta? You talk to him?"

"Yeah, but I don't like him for this," Hannibal said. "First of all, he just doesn't feel like a guy who would kill for money. Besides, he has a solid alibi for the time Wash was attacked, and for that matter so does his bodyguard, Cramer. Alibis we could easily check if we wanted to."

"So we're still in the same place," Rissik said. "Who had a motive to kill both Monroe and his wife?"

"And Jason," Cindy added.

"No motive there," Rissik said. "They killed him just cause it was convenient. We are dealing with a cold blooded son of a bitch."

Cindy nodded, crossed her arms and leaned back against the brick column at the end of the driveway. "How about just a cold blooded bitch? Did he have another woman in his life? She had a man. He might have been playing the same game. A jealous woman might kill the wife to hurt him, and then if she was scorned she might kill him."

"If he had a girlfriend, he'd let her in," Rissik said, nodding. "That gets us around the whole alarm thing."

"Irene told me he had a woman on the side," Hannibal said, staring in the direction of the shopping center. "And when he was drunk Wash said something about being pretty wild in his younger days, even hinted there might be kids out there somewhere."

"All that's real pretty theory," Rissik said. "But I haven't found even a hint of anybody Monroe felt close enough to, to tell stuff like that. And if there was any evidence in his house there sure ain't now. How could we even confirm he had a girl, let alone find out who it was?"

Out of nowhere, Cindy said, "Hamilton Burger."

"What?"

She grinned and pointed at Rissik. "I kept thinking you reminded me of somebody but I couldn't pin it down. In the old Perry Mason TV show. The District Attorney he was always in court with was Hamilton Burger. That's who you remind me of."

"I was just starting to like you," Rissik said with a straight face, "and now you're going to start insulting me?"

Hannibal was shaking his head. "It can't be this hard. Once I got Wash to open up, his mouth never stopped running. He talked constantly, mostly about himself. There must be somebody he confided in."

"Say, didn't you tell me he had a personal assistant?" Cindy asked.

"Sure. Kevin Larson. I talked to him. He didn't have much to offer."

"But that was when Monroe was alive," Cindy said. "He might have been thought he needed to protect his old boss. I'm just saying, if you've got no friends and you're going to confide in anybody…"

Hannibal nodded. "You might just have a point, babe. I might not have asked all the right questions."

"You realize you'll have to be the one breaking this ugly news, right?" Rissik said, waving at the remains of the house. Hannibal sighed and gave a slow nod. Cindy took his hand.

"Don't worry, honey. We can do this together."

Kevin's expression was wary when he opened the door. He wore a dark gray conservative suit and tie. Hannibal realized he must have just returned from an early church service.

"Mr. Jones. What brings you back around here?"

"Well, honestly Kevin I need your help," Hannibal said. "And I'm afraid I have some rather bad news."

At the same moment the two men looked past each other. Hannibal felt Kevin's eyes slip past him, noticing for the first time that his visitor was not alone. For his part, Hannibal spotted Vera at the other end of the living room. Her navy blue dress and three inch heels made her look older than he knew she was.

"Don't just stand there, Kevin," she called. "Invite them in." After quick introductions the four settled at the kitchen table with glasses of iced tea.

"You said something about bad news?" Vera asked. "Does that mean you've found Irene? I had a bad feeling about this from the start."

Hannibal pulled his glasses off. Vera stared into his eyes. Hannibal caught her Sunday scent, a timeless musk. Kevin's eyes were low and hooded. Hannibal took a deep breath. Under the table, Cindy squeezed his hand.

"Three's no news about Mrs. Monroe I'm afraid. But Wash... Mr. Monroe... I'm afraid there was a fire. His house completely destroyed."

"And Mr. Monroe?" Vera asked.

"I'm afraid he was inside."

"Oh Lord Jesus," Vera said, her hand sliding over her husband's.

After a sip of tea Kevin said, "We appreciate you coming to tell us in person. Not the kind of thing you want to find out about in the newspaper, you know?"

"You were close," Cindy said.

"No better people to work for," Kevin said, sliding one of his strong hands back over his head.

"We're trying to find out who might have wanted to hurt them," Hannibal said. "I know this is tough, but I thought Wash might have spoken to you in confidence. We haven't found any friends..."

Kevin spread his hands on the cool pressed wood of the table top. "Mr. Monroe didn't really have any friends. And he didn't talk to me like that either. Don't get me wrong, he was good to me but he was still the boss and I was the worker, you know."

Hannibal did know. People like Wash kept the hired help in their place, even when they didn't mean to. It had been a shot in the gloomy dark of this case. The room fell into silence and he was starting to figure out how they would gracefully leave when Cindy turned to Vera.

"Girls aren't like that," she said in a matter-of-fact tone. "And you look to me like your relationship with Irene was different. Maybe Mr. Monroe confided in her and she in you."

Vera sucked in a breath. "We talked about a lot, but I don't remember anything about anybody that might have wanted to hurt them. If anybody was after them he would only…"

Vera's eyes snapped to her husband. Kevin stared back and Hannibal sensed that telepathy that some married couples develop over time. They seemed to nod to each other in veiled understanding.

"I might know one person Wash would have confided in," Vera said, still looking at Kevin.

"You're thinking of Manny Hernandez," Kevin said. Then to Hannibal, "Did you know that Mr. Monroe used to have a business partner back in the day?"

"In fact, Wash introduced me to him," Hannibal said. Of course, at the time Hannibal viewed him as a suspect, not a source of good intel. Now it occurred to him that Manny might be a resource he had not put to best use.

"I think Vera's right, Mr. Jones," Kevin said. "If you're looking to learn about Wash's past that's the boy who could fill you in."

"Well, thank you both so much for the help." Hannibal stood up and everyone else followed suit. Kevin gave him a strong, firm handshake. He hesitated when he turned to Vera but Cindy stepped in, giving the other woman a warm hug.

Once out the door Hannibal speed walked toward his car, anxious to get back into action. Cindy had to run to catch him at his car door.

"So what's next?" she asked. "Going to get the police to pick up this Hernandez for questioning?"

"He won't tell them a thing," Hannibal said. "But he'll talk to me." Then he gave Cindy a one armed hug. "Hey, you were really good in there. Thanks."

But pulling the passenger door open, he looked into her fawn brown eyes and let his gaze wander down her body, reminding himself that she was not a policeman or a detective, but a lawyer.

"I'll drop you back at the hotel, then head into the city."

"Nuh-uh. In for a penny, in for a pound." She looked up at him with her jaw set. "Honey, I need to see this through with you. Unless you think it will be too dangerous. Is this guy a thug? Are you expecting a shootout?"

"No," Hannibal said. "But then, I never expect a shootout."

Columbia Heights was a quieter neighborhood on Sunday, and Hannibal found a parking space on the same block as the restaurant. Cindy slipped her arm through his as they walked toward Hernandez's legal business. Not only was Hannibal surprised at how few people he saw on the street, but by the apparent shift in their ethnicity.

"Where do you suppose everybody is?" He asked. "All I see is white folks."

"You kill me, honey," Cindy said, allowing a giggle to bubble up out of her. "You're the most observant man I've ever met, but sometimes you can't see anything. It's barely two o'clock. The Hispanic community is at Mass, and most of the black community is still in church, having a lot more fun than their Latin brothers and sisters."

The aroma of peppers and garlic wafted out at them as they approached the restaurant's bright red and green door. Cindy's unexpected smile told Hannibal that his mission might not be as grim as he expected.

"Taberna Pacifico? Is this where you're bringing me?"

"This is Manny Hernandez's club. You know the place?"

"Good food and great salsa music," she said. "Always a good time. I came here a couple of times with..."

Her mouth opened but no name came forth. Hannibal guessed the missing name. He would never go clubbing with her again.

"Come on," he said. "You're not a stranger to this place. Maybe that connection will help us get some answers." He pulled the door open and stepped into the dismal dining area first. He wondered how this hollow space could ever be a place of joy, song and dance. After a quick look around he moved toward the back room until the same grim bouncer stepped out in front of him.

"I'm not looking for trouble," Hannibal said, his hands open and in plain sight. "Please just tell Manny that I've got some news that he'll want to get in person."

Hannibal heard a few words in Spanish from behind the bouncer, and then Hernandez appeared. He stood to the other man's side, but five or six feet behind him. He wore a well-cut suit with narrow lapels and cuffs. His arms crossed in the universal sign of annoyance, of being closed to whomever or whatever was coming.

"What is this news that is so important?"

Cindy took a step forward and bowed her head slightly. She fired off a rush of Spanish. Hannibal didn't catch anything beyond, "Buenos dias, Senor Hernandez" and the name Fernando Lamas. Hernandez's expression showed surprise but only for an instant. Then his hard expression softened and he offered a subtle half-smile. After considering with lips pursed for another second, he snapped his head toward his office, signaling for them to follow. The bouncer swung to the side like an iron gate, allowing them to pass. As they passed him Hannibal looked at Cindy with both hands raised palm up and his shoulders up. Cindy winked and answered his unspoken question.

"I told him that he would want to receive this important news privately, and that you didn't tell me he looked so much like Fernando Lamas."

In the small office Hannibal made the formal introductions. Hernandez took Cindy's hand and kissed it. The desk was cleaned off, and Hernandez pulled the chair out and waited. Cindy smiled at him and turned herself to settle gently on to it as he pushed it in. Then he pulled a wine bottle out of a small refrigerator on the other side of the room.

"Now, Mr. Jones, what is this news that is so bad that you must bring this charming young lady to my restaurant to cushion the blow when you break it to me?"

Hannibal cleared his throat. "You remember that Wash and I originally came here for your help to find out who killed Irene. Well I'm afraid whoever it was doubled back and finished the job. Wash's house burned down last night with him trapped inside."

Hernandez turned the corkscrew until it was fully seated. Staring ahead at the wall he pulled the cork upward with slow, steady pressure until it surrendered with a subtle pop and released a surprising fragrance into the air. It reminded Hannibal of toast, or maybe smoked ham.

"I couldn't trust that little bastard any farther than I could throw the Washington Monument," he said. "He'd have sold me into slavery for a hundred dollars and a good cigar. But I sure loved that gimpy hustler."

"You seem to be as close to a friend as Wash ever had," Hannibal said, leaning back against the desk. "If he confided in anyone it was you."

"If he did, it was because I know how to hold onto information."

"We're not asking you to break any confidences," Hannibal said. "We're hoping you can tell us who would have wanted them both dead."

Hernandez drew three wine glasses from a cabinet with surprising solemnity and filled them half way with the dense purple liquid. He handed glasses to his guests and waited for Cindy to sip before he did. Hannibal tasted it too, and found it dry but impressive. He was no expert but the glow on Cindy's face told him it must be good.

"This is a cabernet, Senor Hernandez?" she asked more than stated. Still it brought a smile to Hernandez' face.

"Cabernet Sauvignon," he replied. "A Vega Sicilia Reserva Especial. And please, my friends call me Manny."

"Thank you, Manny. And my friends call me Cindy." She glanced toward Hannibal, but he nodded to her to continue. It seemed clear that Hernandez would rather speak with her, which Hannibal found quite understandable.

"Manny, we wondered if perhaps a jealous woman might be behind the deaths of your friend and his wife. We understand that Mr. Monroe was..."

"A player?" Hernandez supplied. "Yeah, Wash was a bit of a dog but, hey, that's what men do, you know?"

"So there was a girlfriend," Cindy said.

"What? No." Hernandez pointed at the second chair, waiting for Hannibal to refuse with a shake of his head before dropping into it. "His wife, now she had another man in her life, a boyfriend on the side. Bitch. No, Wash never saw the same girl twice. Just catting around, you know? Nothing like a relationship."

Cindy's lips pressed together, Hannibal assumed to keep her annoyance in. She would not see that this was better or more noble, and for that matter neither did Hannibal. But he had heard it before and was trained not to react emotionally when questioning a witness. Support them, encourage them, and let them talk. That was his style. He took a big swallow of his wine, despite the fact that red wine never appealed to him.

"Are you saying that Wash never once got close to any girl except Irene? A guy like him?"

"Well, years ago," Hernandez said. Then he seemed to focus on the opposite wall, as if an invisible screen there was playing the past in high definition. He stared and drank and smiled. "Yeah, there was this one girl. Damn, I've known that little hustler for a long time. Yeah, before there was Irene there was Sarah. And she turned my boy inside out."

"And where was that?" Hannibal asked.

"Oh, hell, this is down in Charlottesville," Hernandez said. "We was kids back then. But he sure had it bad for that girl. They were together for years."

"You make it sound serious," Cindy said, winking at Hannibal, "but I guess this girl couldn't quite set the hook."

Hernandez took a long, close look at Cindy, as if to make sure she was who he thought she was. "Okay, I'll tell you straight, Cindy. Sarah, she was a looker with a very fine body. A lot like you, if you don't mind me saying so, but maybe a little more, eh, up top and in the bottom. Smart and smooth as any girl going to U. VA. But she was from the street, you know? And she wasn't ready to forget that. Now Irene, she was the real deal, and that was the shit Wash was looking for, you know. The right accessory to get him into the right place in society."

"And she was a white girl," Hannibal said. "I'm betting Sarah wasn't."

"Sarah? Perfect ebony skin, like Mary J. Blige," Hernandez said, refilling Cindy's glass, then Hannibal's and then his own. "But you right, Esai, Wash always played the long game and his plan called for a white girl with debutante style. One day it was Sarah, the next day she was just gone."

"What was Sarah's last name?" Cindy asked. Hannibal grimaced.

"What, you think you'll find her in the phone book? Oh, you're thinking she drove up here, shot Irene and set Wash's house on fire. No, the girl didn't have that kind of hate in her."

"Where were her people from?" Hannibal asked.

"Jamaica, I think," Hernandez said. "Or St. Thomas. One of them West Indian islands. No, her name was Thomas. Sarah Thomas. Don't know that's still it. The three of us pulled some nice bits back in the day. But you can't think she'd do this. If she was going to come after Wash it would have happened years ago."

Hannibal wasn't going to tell him that any number of things could make a woman hire a hit man years after a man dumped her. Aloud he said, "Sure would like to talk to her, though. Sounds like she knew Wash pretty well. She might know something useful. And she might want to know what happened. Any idea where she ended up?"

"Even if I did, I'm not sure she'd want me to go spreading it around."

Cindy emptied her glass, stood slowly and smoothed her skirt. Hannibal saw the change but wasn't sure if Hernandez did. But her face slipped through a subtle transformation and in five seconds his seductive chica was gone, replaced by the lawyer who had faced down government agencies and big businesses in court so many times.

"This can go two ways, Manuel," she said. "Down one path, we go to the police with news of a woman who might have information concerning three recent murders."

"Three?" Hernandez' eyes narrowed. He must have been in court at some point in the past, because he certainly recognized her tone.

"Yes," Cindy said with unnatural calm. "One of my coworkers was caught in the middle of this mess. Collateral damage as they say in war. Anyway, we give the police a name, a sketchy description, a college and an approximate attendance period. Oh, and naturally we'd have to name our source. They go thrashing around, as the police are prone to do, question everyone they can find, flash badges all over the place, harass her family and friends and finally hunt her down. She probably has nothing to contribute to their investigation but they make her life miserable anyway because they're frustrated."

The corner of Hernandez' lip curls and he looks at Hannibal. Their eyes exchange silent conversation.

*Your woman?*

*Yeah, and she's more than either of us can handle.*

Hernandez returned his focus to Cindy. "And the other way?"

"Well, down the other path, you tell us where you think we can find her. Hannibal and I speak to her quietly. Your name never comes up. If, as I suspect, all we get is background information we just go away and the police never hear about that conversation, or this one. That's the beauty of working with a private investigator, after all."

Hernandez raises the bottle again. Hannibal shook his head, but Cindy accepted a refill. He emptied the bottle into his own glass and stared at the dark red liquid as he spoke.

"You, chica, are a dangerous woman." After seven seconds he continued. "I heard she married, but that could be just a rumor. I do know that she never left the state. The last I heard, she was running a gentlemen's club over in Arlington. There ain't that many so she shouldn't be too hard to find. Good enough?"

Cindy nodded. "Thank you for your time, Manny. If this lead works out, I'm pretty sure we can keep your name out of this."

Hannibal held the door for her and was about to follow when Hernandez called his name. Hannibal stopped to look back over his shoulder.

"One other condition for that info I just gave you," Hernandez said. "You got to call me when this is all over. I got a feeling about you. You don't quit until the job is done, do you? Well, I want to know what happened to Wash. He was a shit there at the end, but we were partners for a long time."

Hannibal nodded and walked on. Outside he saw Cindy squinting to find the car. After the dimness of the club the outdoor brightness took on a surreal quality. They didn't speak again until they were leaning back in their seats and the engine was murmuring under the hood.

"That wasn't what I expected," Cindy said. "Maybe there is a kind of honor among thieves."

"Did you believe him? The whole time we were in there I was reminding myself that I was listening to a world class con man. Was any of that sincere?"

"I don't know," Cindy said. "That was a mighty expensive bottle of Spanish wine he popped, and that was before we asked the hard questions. I think he was really mourning the loss of a friend."

Hannibal nodded as they pulled away from the curb. "Well, I don't really care as long as his lead pans out. Right now we have some research to do and since we're in the District already I'd rather do it at my own computer."

"What? You mean you don't know all the gentlemen's clubs in Arlington?"

## -15-

Four days had passed since Hannibal had last pulled into his traditional space across the street from his apartment. The sky was as clear there in his neighborhood in Southeast Washington as it was in the rest of the city he had just driven through, but somehow the sun didn't seem to shine as brightly. Overarching trees certainly weren't the cause of the difference. Even the older trees on the block were stunted and wispy. But the street, and even the buildings on either side of it, were dark with the accumulated dirt and air pollutants driven into them over the last century. And the narrow street and buildings crowded together in rows combined to cast one side of the street into shadow at any given time of the day except noon.

Hannibal wondered how many of his neighbors missed home as much as he did after just a few days.

Ray Santiago, who lived upstairs from Hannibal, stepped out onto the stoop as Hannibal approached. Hannibal smiled and nodded as Cindy sprinted past him and up the sandstone steps. She flew into Ray's arms and clutched him to her. Ray was a little shorter, but stocky enough to lift her off her feet in the hug. Hannibal wondered if she would crush the breath out of her father's body.

After a long moment Hannibal slipped past them and led them into his office. After the long embrace an awkward silence grew up between Cindy and Ray. Hannibal filled it by busying himself with the details of grinding coffee beans, fetching water and getting the coffee pot going. When Cindy walked over to look out the window, Ray stared after her, and then turned to Hannibal.

"Is somebody going to tell me what's going on?"

Hannibal moved to his desk and started his computer as if he didn't hear. Ray turned to Cindy and said something in Spanish. His voice was soft and low. Cindy responded in the same tone. Ray repeated his question, with just a touch more of an edge in his voice.

"I'm sure Hannibal has already told you the important parts," Cindy said in English, never taking her eyes off the car across the street.

Ray shook his head. "Are you nuts, girl? Hannibal wouldn't tell me shit. But I know when there's something wrong with my little girl and I want to know what the hell it is."

Hannibal kept his nose in his monitor, but out the corner of his eye he saw Cindy's head pop up as if jerked by a noose. She looked quickly over her shoulder at Hannibal before turning all the way to face her father.

"Papa, I'm really sorry I didn't come to you, but you mustn't be upset with Hannibal. I just wasn't in any condition to tell anyone about the friend I lost, or even more that I let myself get swindled out of the money."

"The money?" Ray asked, stepping closer. "What money?"

"All the money," Cindy said with a heavy sigh. "Papa it's all gone. All the climbing, all the progress I made, and now I'm back to square one."

Ray chewed his lower lip. "This is about money? Come. Sit down." Ray guided Cindy into the visitor's chair and squatted on his haunches in front of her. Hannibal guessed that this was how their conversations were staged when she was ten years old. Ray watched Cindy's eyes. Cindy stared at Ray's shoes. Her face clouded up.

"I'm sorry I let you down, Papa," she said. "I know you came to this country with nothing and scraped all your life just so I could make something of myself. I was there, Papa, I had the brass ring in my hand, and I got greedy and stupid and let it get snatched away from me."

"How can a girl be so smart and so stupid at the same time," Ray said, shaking his head. "What, you think the path to success is a set of stairs you just walk up? You think you fell down the stairs and can't get up. Let me tell you, Cintia. It's more like a game of chutes and ladders. That's the way it is for everybody. Even Donald Trump has been dead broke a couple times. Nobody's disappointed in you but you." He turned to Hannibal, "Right?"

"What?" Hannibal looked up, surprised to have been pulled into their private conversation. Ray glared at him, clearly expecting instant support. "Of course, Ray. You're right. I told her so before. But I think it means a lot more coming from you."

Hannibal returned his eyes to the screen. He was trying to so hard to stay out of their moment that he was unaware of Ray's approach until he was standing in front of the desk.

"So what are you working on that's so important, Chico?"

Hannibal looked up, as if he had been caught cheating on a test. "Me? Oh, I have to try to find this woman who might have had a motive for these murders."

"Murder case, huh? Well if the guy's dead he could wait. I think Cintia needs you right now."

"What she needs right now is for me to close this case," Hannibal said. "And it's murders, plural. That friend that Cindy mentioned that she lost? He's one of the victims."

"Oh." Ray stopped for a moment, looking from Hannibal to Cindy and back. Then he cleared his throat said in a lower tone, "You do know what she needs, don't you? You think a woman did it?"

"We had a couple other suspects, but right now this woman seems like our best lead."

"You got an address?"

Hannibal chuckled. "It never works like that, Ray. But we got this lead from another suspect we've pretty much cleared. He thinks she might work at a club in Arlington."

"A club?" Ray asked.

"Yes, a, er, a gentleman's club."

"Class girl or street girl?" Ray asked. Cindy looked at him, her mouth falling open.

"She graduated from U.VA," Hannibal said.

"Oh, well save yourself some computer time, Paco," Ray said. "She's got to be working at The Lucent. There's only a couple of these places around here. The Grill is a dive and Dauphine out in Springfield closed a while back."

"Daddy? Are you a regular at one of these places?"

Ray shook his head and stared at his daughter. "And if I was, would it be any business of yours, little girl?"

"I didn't mean... I was just surprised, that's all."

Ray chuckled. "Not my scene, really. But hey, I'm a cab driver, remember? I get calls to those places all the time. And I can tell a lot by who goes, you know? Now the Lucent City Restaurant, it's kind of an upscale gentleman's club, and for sure they got the prettiest girls around here."

"Well I'll be damned," Hannibal said. "A strip club hidden in Arlington. I thought they were all down in Richmond or Virginia Beach."

"Well, yeah, they got a ton of them down there," Ray said. "But don't make no assumptions here, Paco. First of all, this place serves a decent steak. And they ain't really strippers, more go-go dancers."

"I think the term they use today is exotic dancers, Papa."

"Whatever," Ray said. "But the other thing is, it ain't hid. It's right on the main drag, around the corner from Route One, in the middle of Crystal City."

"It sounds like Sarah Thomas might not be too hard to find," Hannibal said, rising and reaching for coffee. "Wonder if these places are open on Sundays."

"What, you think guys don't want to see girls work a pole on Sunday?" Ray asked, pulling his favorite mug from a shelf.

"Never really thought about it," Hannibal said, filling both their mugs. "Guess I can follow up on this lead right away."

"You're not thinking of going to this place," Cindy said, stepping between the two men. Hannibal tipped his head slightly to glare at her.

"You want to rephrase that question, miss?"

Surprise moved quickly across Cindy's face. After a brief glance at her father her expression softened and she placed a hand on Hannibal's arm.

"What I meant was, you're not thinking of going to this place without me, are you?"

Ray snorted and Hannibal worked to stifle a chuckle. "Well of course not, babe," Hannibal said. "It sounds like a good place for dinner and a little investigating. The only question is, are you dressed right for the place?"

"Hey, my little girl don't own that kind of clothes," Ray said.

In fact, Cindy chose the basic black mid-length dress with pearls and her highest pumps. Hannibal had driven her back to her own townhome in Alexandria so she could get ready and watched the whole process with more amusement than lust. When she had changed her choice of earrings five times and gotten her hair just right they returned to the Volvo. But as Hannibal opened the door for Cindy he froze.

He was watching her face and saw her smile replaced by a look of curiosity. She was looking over his shoulder at something unexpected. Still, she sat down so he figured whatever she saw was not threatening. He closed the door and casually looked up the block.

The man walking toward them slowed his pace when Hannibal looked toward him. He was too far away to identify, not far from the corner. Hannibal would not have given the man a second thought if his face had not been obscured by the hood of a gray George Mason University sweatshirt. Of course there were millions of such garments in the area. This could be anybody.

But just to be sure Hannibal took a few steps toward the man in the hoodie. That man stopped, turned and retraced his steps. He walked quickly but didn't run. When he rounded the corner, Hannibal broke into a sprint. His heart pounded as a feeling of déjà vu rushed over him. It was as if Irene Monroe had just dropped to the ground in front of him. He reached the corner in seconds and drew his pistol.

The street was empty. There was no one in sight on the entire block. His quarry could have stepped into any of a number of doors, or slipped into one of several cars. Swallowing a mixture of frustration, curiosity and slight embarrassment he holstered his weapon and slowly returned to his car.

"Want to tell me what that was about?" Cindy asked as he slid behind the wheel.

"Thought I saw someone I recognized," Hannibal said, hoping Cindy had not seen him draw his pistol. "Did you know that guy?"

"No," Cindy said. "And I thought I knew all my neighbors. That's why he caught my attention."

"Probably nothing," Hannibal said. He fastened his seat belt and settled in for the ten minute drive to the edge of the state. In those four miles Washington Street became Route One and then Jefferson Davis Highway as they rolled into the non-town of Crystal City.

Crystal City is a commercial area in Arlington, but doesn't quite qualify as a neighborhood. Sitting within walking distance of Reagan National Airport, Crystal City might best be described as an urban village, composed of corporate offices, hotels, shops, restaurants and high-rise apartment buildings. It's also just south of Washington D.C. and straddles the busy main road into the city from Virginia. That makes the area rather unfriendly to pedestrians, at least on the surface. However, its core of offices, hotels, stores and residential buildings is linked not just by narrow landscaped parks but by an extensive underground shopping and entertainment complex with connecting corridors in all directions.

Hannibal was surprised to find the Lucent on street level, one of the many inconspicuous storefronts on one of the side streets. Evening was just rolling into the area, and foot traffic was heavier than he expected. With Cindy on his arm and no idea what to expect he pulled open the door and stepped inside.

## The Pyramid Deception

His first impression was how clean and bright the club was, but that may have been exaggerated by his preconceived notions. It was indeed set up like a middle class restaurant, at least half of it was. The far half was more of a bar with two stages. One was already occupied by a shapely young Asian lady who moved more like a ballerina than a stripper.

"I thought we could get a meal before the entertainment began," Cindy said in a stage whisper as the hostess approached.

"On Sundays the dancers start at four." The brunette who met them at the door wore a broad smile and a modified bikini. A mini skirt covered the bottom part, but Hannibal thought her smile was bigger. "My name is Tahnee," she said. "Welcome to The Lucent. We have no cover charge, but there is a one drink minimum per person, and the use of cameras, including camera phones, is not permitted. May I show you to a table?"

Hannibal nodded and Tahnee escorted them through the dining area. The music was not quite loud enough to be annoying, but it was upbeat and driving in its way. When they reached their table Hannibal turned to hand Tahnee his card.

"While we're here we'd like a moment with an old friend, a Miss Sarah Thomas. Just give her that card and tell her I have some important news for her concerning her past connections. She'll know what I mean."

He saw her eyes widen for less than a second before she recaptured her composure. "I'll be happy to ask around but I'm not sure I know her. We all pretty much use stage names here so I can't be sure. In the meantime, would you like drinks?"

Hannibal requested a bottle of Riesling and settled in to scan the menu. He couldn't help but notice that Tahnee had seated them so that he faced the stage.

"She was nice," Cindy said.

"You're nicer. Want an appetizer?"

"They're all basic bar food," she said. "How about some stuffed jalapeños? Seems appropriate."

Hannibal agreed. They ordered when Tahnee returned but there was no mention of Sarah Thomas. He saw no reason to press the point. If she wasn't there they would still just enjoy their dinner. If she was there but didn't want to talk to them, there was little to be done about it. The lead seemed slim anyway. Hannibal almost hoped it wouldn't pan out. Waiting for their food, sipping wine and biting into stuffed hot peppers, he realized that this was the first truly natural and relaxed moment he had had with Cindy in a week. Even peeking over her shoulder at the entertainment, her sense of humor seemed to have returned.

"Hey, she's hot," she said. "What do they need all these big screen plasmas for? Must be insulting to the strippers."

"Well if you'd tear your eyes away from the bootie for a second you'd notice they're all on sports events, just like any other bar."

"Doesn't seem fair," Cindy said with a smirk. "You don't see them showing porn on the screen at a Wizards game. Now if I was up there working that pole..."

"No one would notice the TVs."

A change of dancers made Hannibal notice the people around him. The new girl was white, as were the great majority of the patrons. All were well dressed, almost all were couples, and they were quieter than he had expected. Maybe they regarded this as just another dining spot. He wondered if anyone ever came into the Lucent Restaurant without knowing it was a strip club until it was too late to gracefully back out.

Their entrees arrived quickly, and Cindy commented, "I'm surprised you didn't go for the fried oysters in this place."

"Sorry, babe, but it seemed more appropriate to order the strip steak."

He liked the heavy silverware but even without it the knife would have glided through his medium rare 16 ounce steak, nicely blackened at his request. It was as crunchy as he hoped on the outside and very moist within. After the first bite he added pepper from the mill and passed on any kind of sauce.

Cindy's face told him she was equally surprised at the seafood on her combo platter. The broiled scallops, she told him, were how you judged a chef's hand with seafood. Watching her more than the flexible performer behind her, Hannibal remembered why he had gotten drawn into this case, and why he was drawn into her life.

"This is what I wanted to see more than anything. You looking happy."

"Happy?" Cindy paused to chew a shrimp. "I don't know. I'm still angry. And hurting. In mourning I guess."

Hannibal reached across the table to cover her left hand with his. "Perfectly normal, babe. Friends are hard to lose."

Cindy stopped with a forkful of crab cake half way to her mouth and looked up to meet Hannibal's eyes. "And there's guilt, Hannibal. I'm so ashamed of myself. When I was sitting in that hotel room alone after hearing that Jason was really gone, I realized that I was mourning the money more than him. That's why I almost...what I almost did. Now I realize that life has to go on. And after tonight I'm going to let you do what you do. I'm not a detective. Where I belong is in that law office taking care of my clients, and tomorrow morning that's where I'll be."

Hannibal smiled and was about to say something about people doing what they were born to do when an approaching figure distracted him. It was another of the bikini clad wait staff. This was the first woman of color he had seen aside from the guests. She was average height but looked like some giant had gripped her waist and squeezed much of her body up and down, leaving her in an exaggerated hourglass shape. Her smooth skin, straight black hair and exotic eyes spoke of a Polynesian background. When she stopped at the table she made a point of looking at both of them.

"Hello. My name is Myca."

"Of course it is," Hannibal said.

"Ms. Thomas asked me to check to make sure your meal was satisfactory."

"I have to say the steak was excellent. Cindy?"

"A surprisingly good meal," she said. "Usually at a dinner theater, either the food or the show is disappointing. But not this time."

Myca stifled a well-rehearsed giggle. "The chef, and the performers will be pleased. Ms. Thomas also asked if you could tell me a little more about the message you had for her."

"I'm afraid that message is for her ears alone," Hannibal said. "But you could tell her that it concerns George Washington Monroe."

Myca nodded and appeared to do a little calculus in her head. Then she refreshed her smile and said, "Please follow me. And don't worry about the check. Ms. Thomas will take care of that."

"That's very generous," Hannibal said standing and reaching into his pocket, "but I still need to leave a tip. The service was excellent."

"Yes, what happened to Tahnee?" Cindy asked.

"Change of shifts," Myca said. "We rotate." She nodded toward one of the stages. Tahnee was giving an energetic dance performance, whipping the nearby male patrons into a subdued frenzy.

"Rotate," he said with a smile. "You do indeed."

Myca led them to a door that was obscured by a sheer curtain hanging in front of it. After guiding them through she led them down a hallway to a small service elevator. Hannibal and Cindy entered but Myca stayed in the hall, pushed a button and waved to them as the doors closed.

"The whole speakeasy feel of these places just doesn't go away, does it?" Cindy said.

Hannibal didn't say anything, but his left hand was halfway to his shoulder holster when the elevator doors opened on the lower level. They stepped out into a room that was a little bigger than Hannibal's living room but was set up as an office. The furniture, conservative but not antique, rested on a dark brown carpet. The room smelled of cinnamon and vanilla. At the far end of the room a woman sat at a computer with her back to them, apparently handling some correspondence. Her fingers tapped the keys with the deft expertise of an executive secretary.

"Hello?" Cindy called. "We were looking for a Sarah Thomas."

The woman spun toward them on her wheeled chair. "You've found her. Now who are you?"

"My name is Cindy Santiago."

"And I'm Hannibal Jones."

"Yes I know," Sarah said. "That's why you're here. So what's on your mind?"

The woman was close to Hannibal's height, near six feet tall, with raven hair in waves resting on her shoulders. Her smile challenged him while she pulled out and lit a cigarette.

"Ms. Thomas, I have news regarding your ex-husband, George Washington Monroe. He would want you to know."

"Know what?" she asked. Her beauty was fully matured and her skin was as dark as ebony. After meeting a brunette named Tahnee and another woman named Myca, Hannibal wondered if Sarah had danced as Onyx.

"He would want you to know that he's dead."

Sarah took a deep drag on her slender cigarette and sat back on the desk. "Wash is dead?"

"Wash is dead. I believe he was murdered."

Sarah pointed toward the small round meeting table, inviting them to sit. She again filled her lungs with smoke. She breathed it out in a long, slow stream. She reached back to the desk and pushed buttons on the phone. A young woman answered.

"Bourbon," Sarah said. Then she stepped slowly toward the table on heels that might have frightened Tina Turner. She looked at Cindy, then Hannibal and said, "Thank you. Thank you for coming instead of calling. You are an exception among your gender, Mr. Jones. You are all that people say you are."

A dancer/waitress entered carrying a tray. She placed it on the table, set a glass in front of each of the guests and left one in front of an empty chair. She smiled at the guests, nodded toward

Sarah, and vanished out the door. Sarah poured for the three of them and settled into her chair.

"How do you know Hannibal?"

Sarah looked at Hannibal. "She with you?" When Hannibal nodded, Sarah turned to Cindy. "You know what you got, right?"

"Yes, I believe I do."

Sarah smiled and leaned back. "Girls on the street know Jones. They know if they get into trouble he doesn't worry about who they are or what they do. And they know he doesn't ask for specials or freebies or payment in kind."

Hannibal nodded his thanks. "I haven't found a lot of people who were close to Wash," Hannibal said. "I'm hoping you can help me find out who took his life. Have you been in touch with him recently?"

"I'm afraid I haven't seen Wash since the day he gave me the money to set this place up," Sarah said, swirling the liquor in her glass. "That was five years ago."

"Five years." Hannibal repeated her words, lifting his glass and inhaling the aroma from the snifter but not drinking yet. "About the time he committed to Irene."

Sarah gave a bitter grin. "Severance pay."

"You couldn't have been with Wash all that time," Cindy said.

"No, not all that time. We were together for a while, then I left Wash for a few years because I thought I could see where his life was going. I married a man I thought would take care of me. All he ever gave me was a hard time and three little mouths to feed. When he took off I kind of floated back to Wash. We had some more good times but then he set his sights on a younger girl, so he needed me and mine to disappear."

"I see," Hannibal said. "Severance pay." Cindy shook her head and tasted her bourbon.

"Yeah, but I didn't get mad," Sarah said. "I had pretty much wasted my life up to then, but I took his cash and my degree and my knowledge of what men really care about, and I started this place. The Lucent has been profitable since year one."

"It took me a while to get the name," Cindy said. "Lucent, meaning luminous, right? Also short for pellucid, a synonym for clear or transparent, not hiding anything. Like your girls."

"I'm impressed," Sarah said. "You picked up the second meaning, but maybe you missed the historic context."

"Enlighten us," Hannibal said.

Sarah took a small sip of bourbon. "Well, the first building that opened here back in the sixties was called Crystal House and it had this huge crystal chandelier in the lobby. After that they all copied it. Crystal Gateway on that side, Crystal Towers over here. I didn't want to do that so I called this place Lucent, as in translucent, to kind of resonate with the crystal imagery. Probably nobody noticed but me."

"You started a business while still a young mother?" Cindy said. "I for one am impressed."

"You don't know the half of it, sister," Sarah said, waving the thought away with a hand. "I figured I could use a little help so I got involved with another man. We got married, and he did help recruit the talent, but Sid got too friendly with the hired help and I had to toss him out on his ass."

"So there you were," Hannibal said with as little emotion as possible. "Alone, raising a family while trying to get a business off the ground, and all because Wash Monroe kicked you to the curb for a younger woman. A white girl at that. You must have come to resent him as time passed."

"Resent him? Wash was a Godsend in those days." Sarah tipped her glass up, emptying the contents down her throat. "Look, Wash may not have given a damn about me, but he felt responsible. He made sure the kids had what they needed no matter what. Even paid for surgery when one of them needed it. And when they were old enough, he made sure all four of my boys had jobs, either working for him or for somebody who owed him. Took a lot of the weight off me while I was trying to make it. I don't know if anybody else will mourn that man, but you can bet your ass I will." She slammed her glass down on the table as if to put an exclamation point on her sentence.

A close look into Sarah's eyes convinced Hannibal that her emotions were real. He was letting a few seconds pass for Sarah to collect herself when Cindy spoke up.

"So who wanted him dead?"

"Damned if I know," Sarah said. "But I sure hope you find the son of a bitch."

Beyond that the three exchanged the pleasantries required by polite society but all three knew the conversation was over. Cindy stood when Hannibal did, they thanked their hostess for her time and stepped into the narrow elevator. The second the doors slid closed, Cindy took Hannibal's arm and spoke in a low tone.

"I guess this was a dead end, but I'm glad we got to talk to her. A life like hers sure gives you perspective. Impressive lady."

Hannibal turned to smile down at her. It was one of the things he loved most about Cindy, her natural tendency to see the best in people. She warmed his heart, and the smile that generated was still there when the elevator doors slid open and a hard black fist drove deep into his stomach.

## -16-

A hand like a catcher's mitt smothered Cindy's scream. Two muscular men squeezed into the narrow box. Cindy's arm, wrapped around Hannibal's right arm, had short-circuited his response to the first punch and his other fist didn't travel far enough to do much damage. He took a couple more solid body blows and a right cross slammed his head back into the wall. Then each of his attackers took one of his arms and half walked half dragged Hannibal's dazed form out of the elevator. He was just conscious enough to curse himself for letting his guard down.

Both attackers, young black men, wore pea coats and jeans and thick work boots. Their body odor fought through their coats to assault Hannibal's nose. He could hear the music of the club muffled by a wall and becoming more and more distant. Both men had strong grips and when Hannibal struggled to free his arms it earned him a sharp shot to the ribs.

They travelled down a narrow hall and out into the cool evening air. When his eyes began to focus Hannibal saw Cindy close behind him. A third man followed too close to her, and Hannibal saw the glint of a stainless steel revolver in his hand.

The thin twilight gave way to the harsh lights of a little-used hotel entrance. Hannibal heard a pair of approaching footsteps. The man at the back tucked his gun into his coat pocket. Hannibal heard the man on his right mumble, "He'll be all right," as if Hannibal were just sick or drunk. He knew the hall wasn't really deserted, but that people inside the Beltway were highly skilled at minding their own business.

In less than a minute they were in one of the underground parking lots that formed an amorphous network beneath Crystal

City. Hannibal knew this was the moment to make his move. The lighting was dim, there were plenty of cars to hide behind and there was no telling when someone might wander through. Given a few minutes to get his head together Hannibal knew he could easily take these three amateurs out.

Then he looked back at Cindy's face. It was the face of terror. Her wooden steps and shallow breaths revealed the predictable reaction of a good, law-abiding citizen who had never had a firearm pointed at them. He could not rely on her to move quickly or well, even if an opportunity came.

The shiny prod at her back was more than a fistful for its owner. The short-barreled .44 Magnum would deafen them all if it went off in the parking garage. More importantly, it was not a weapon that required a great deal of precision. If one of those bullets hit you anywhere, even peripherally, it would throw you to the ground. Against his will, Hannibal pictured Cindy's organs blossoming out of her chest in front of a .44 Magnum round fired at close range. No, putting her at risk of that was out of the questions. Besides, these guys were young, maybe even just big teenagers. They might not think through their reactions to any trouble he caused.

Hannibal offered no resistance, even when one of his escorts slammed him into the side of a small Toyota. Hannibal recognized their vehicle as a Rav 4, a compact Sport Utility Vehicle which, to him, was a contradiction in terms. Then the men holding his arms pulled him upright. Number Three swung into view on the other side of the vehicle, dragging Cindy by a fistful of her hair. Hannibal's gut clenched when he saw that man poke the barrel of his pistol against her temple. Her mouth dropped open but nothing came out but coarse panting. The men holding Hannibal tightened their grips. Now they were waiting for his reaction.

"It's going to be okay," he said, forcing his voice to reflect his words. "They don't really want to hurt you. You're just here so they can control me. We'll be okay as long as they know I won't cause any trouble."

The hands on Hannibal's arms relaxed a bit. The man on his left reached under his jacket and looked disappointed to find no gun under Hannibal's left arm. He smiled when he found it on the other side.

"Southpaw, eh?"

"Yeah, but my right works pretty good too. Want to see?"

The two men locked eyes and for a moment Hannibal thought he might get a chance to do some damage. If he caused enough confusion he might get close enough to Cindy's captor to separate them. But then, that man spoke up in a derisive tone.

"Just get him in the car, Darryl. Don't let him get you going."

Hannibal gave it one more shot. "So this is your brother Darryl, huh? And over here, is this your other brother Darryl?"

That prompted the man on his right to slam a fist into Hannibal's ribs. Then he pulled Hannibal's arms backward and together so Darryl could wrap several layers of duct tape around Hannibal's wrists. Then Darryl opened the Rav 4's back door. His partner shoved Hannibal inside and followed him in. When they were settled the gunman opened the door on the other side and shoved Cindy in. Darryl got behind the wheel. The gunman took the passenger seat, his pistol casually pointed between Hannibal and Cindy. They moved like men who had worked together for a long time.

The little SUV pulled out of the garage and up into the dimming sunlight. When they slowed at the first corner Hannibal wished Cindy would jump out but he knew she wouldn't. She knew that would put Hannibal at risk, just as he knew that any move he made would make her the target. Each would avoid taking risks they might if they were alone, for fear of harm coming to the other. The simplest traps are the most elegant.

The gunman aimed his barrel between the bucket seats at Hannibal's navel and addressed his muscular partner.

"Find his phone, Nas."

"Nas?" Hannibal asked while the beefy man poked into Hannibal's inside jacket pockets. "Really? They named you after a rapper?"

Both men ignored him. The gunman turned his gun an inch to Hannibal's right. "Give me your phone, shorty."

"I don't have one."

"Please," he said, eyes rolling. "A bitch without a phone?" He snatched her purse with his free hand and dumped the contents in his lap. Cindy looked as if she had forgotten she was clutching her handbag until it was yanked out of her hands. The act seemed to hit her harder than having a gun to her head.

"Okay, okay, my phone is in there but you can't have that. I keep my notes, my records, all my contacts and their info in that thing. My whole life is in that device. How dare you?"

The gunman raised the barrel and pressed it forward, inches from Cindy's face. "I dare because I got the gun, bitch. If you didn't hang out with niggers like this you wouldn't be getting your shit snatched."

Cindy ignored the gun, locking eyes with the gunman. "And if you need a gun and two friends to act all tough to a woman, you're the bitch."

Behind the wheel, Daryl snorted. Nas reached between the seats to slap Cindy. He didn't have much leverage and she was still glaring at him after the blow. Hannibal leaned over to push his face between his woman and the pistol.

"Hey! You got a beef with me, bring it to me."

The man sitting next to Hannibal clamped a hand around Hannibal's neck and pulled him back upright.

"We always handle our own beefs," he snarled into Hannibal's ear. "We don't do other people's dirt, or hire ourselves out to…"

"Shut up, Eddie," Darryl said from the driver's seat. His voice was soft but Eddie reacted as if he had been slapped. Hannibal sat back, leaned against Cindy trying to show support, and wondered about what had gone unsaid.

## -17-

Hannibal watched the sun slip toward the horizon on his right while he tried to loosen the tape around his wrists and reviewed the events of the last few days. He had a big pile of facts and a few reasonable suppositions, but none of them led to even a good guess at what he most wanted to know right then. After watching the countryside fly past for the better part of an hour he finally asked.

"All right, I give up. Who are you guys, and why are you so mad at me?"

Eddie pulled off the highway and began to drive around through twisting streets as if he were trying to evade followers. "So you still don't get it, huh?" he said. "You must do so much bad shit you can't keep it all straight. No biggie. When we get to the house I'll lay it all out for you. After all, your bitch ought to know why this is going to be her final resting place too. Yours and hers, like it was almost his."

A cold sweat defied gravity and ran up Hannibal's spine. The neighborhood began to look familiar, even in the gathering twilight. The perfectly groomed lawns held the massive homes back from the narrow street. He recognized a particular brick fronted house with a pillared entryway and enough yard around it that residents would never hear their nearest neighbor scream. As he vehicle crept down the darkening streets Hannibal knew where he was. But he still didn't know why.

Darryl pulled into the driveway that led to the mound of ashes and charred rubble Hannibal had so recently visited. Debris covered most of the footprint of the house, with blackened timbers looking as if they were trying to climb up out of what was once the basement level. On the left, the circular asphalt path led to the remains of a three-car garage, growing up out of the remains like a disembodied limb. Actually only two walls of the garage remained. Darryl took the RAV4 into the grass to pull up behind the little structure. The stand of trees behind the house gave them a certain level of seclusion. When he cut the engine, Darryl turned a grim smile on Hannibal.

"Last stop. Time to get out and face the music."

Eddie popped the door and dragged Cindy out of the car. She stumbled on the uneven ground but quickly righted herself. Nas opened the door on the other side and Hannibal managed to climb out despite his bound hands. He walked around to the other side of the vehicle to face his three captors. Night had fallen hard, without the moon rising. Distant streetlamps lacked the strength or the courage to reach into the darkness that surrounded them. With his back to the tree line Hannibal was a good hundred yards from the street. He might make such a run without getting hit by a poor marksman with a revolver. Cindy, not so much.

"Okay, why here?" Hannibal asked. "Why bring us to the remains of George Monroe's house?"

Darryl offered a hateful smile. "Because the perfect hiding place is the place that's already been searched. The law and the emergency crews have already picked all through this mess, so they know there's nobody else in there. Nobody's going look again. And tomorrow or the next day when they come to gather up all this shit, nobody will notice your two bodies jammed in there under all this crap. You'll just get hauled away with the rest of the trash. Kind of poetic too, don't you think? You made this mess, now you get to be part of it."

Cindy's head snapped back. "What? You think Hannibal did this? Are you high? He was working for the man."

"You stupid bitch," Nas said, waving his gun back and forth between Hannibal and Cindy. "He wasn't working for Wash. He was working for that white bitch, Irene. We thought we got there in time, but I guess she got to the tough guy here before we got to her."

"That was you?" Hannibal asked with genuine surprise. These three didn't feel like drive by shooters or barroom sneak attackers. "What the hell? Irene wasn't a client. I met with her to get information about Wash…"

"Yeah, to kill him," Eddie said, taking a menacing step forward. "First she squeezes Mama out, then she figures to take Papa Wash out and get all his money."

"Whoa!" Cindy shook her head in surprise. "Mama? You guys are Sarah's boys?"

"I can't believe she set us up," Hannibal said. "Does your momma know she raised a pack of thugs?"

Eddie reacted to Hannibal's remark with a hard backhand slap that sent his Oakleys spinning off into the darkness. Hannibal staggered but refused to fall.

"Ain't that some shit?" Darryl said. "A hit man calling US thugs. Well, maybe we have moved some drugs and helped get some losers to repay their debts, but none of us ever killed nobody for money."

"You are on drugs," Cindy said. "You idiots think Hannibal's a killer? He was only talking to Irene to…"

"To set up the hit," Darryl said. "We know how these white girls do. She hung with Wash until she found herself a young lawyer, then she figured to get Wash out of the way. But we got ahead of that shit. They had to go."

"You gunned her down," Hannibal said through clenched teeth. "Right in front of me."

Cindy's mind went elsewhere. "Jason. You assholes killed Jason, didn't you? He never did a thing to you but you murdered him just for kicks. You bastards!"

Cindy had gotten past her anger, perhaps too far past it, Hannibal thought. He needed to get the brothers' attention.

"It wasn't for fun, was it, Darryl? Jason needed to die to cover up the murder, and make me out to be a liar."

"Yeah, that was pretty slick, wasn't it?" Darryl said, nodding. "We had to make out like Irene just ran away with her boyfriend, so he had to disappear. Had the cops going there for a while, didn't we?"

"Enough bullshit," Eddie said. "Let's just get them in the ground."

Hannibal gave it one last shot. "You guys don't have to do this. I'm pretty good at reading people and I think I got to understand your mother during our little chat. She might accept you breaking the law from time to time but trust and believe she would not want her boys to be murderers. And I swear to you, I didn't kill Wash. If you kill me you'll think it's over and you'll never find out who really did it."

"Shut the hell up," Darryl said. He pulled a small automatic out of his coat and a screw-on silencer from his pocket. "Drag your ass over there in what's left of the garage and we'll do this quick and painless. If you've been doing this for a while I'm sure you know how this works."

"Not really. And I suspect you don't either."

Hannibal had been waiting for an opportunity, any small distraction that would give him a chance at survival, or at least offer Cindy a chance. Fate had always thrown him a bone when he needed it, and that was all he prayed for now.

The slim chance came in the form of a car turning the corner toward them. For an instant, headlights racked across the brothers' backs. They would ignore it if allowed to. But Hannibal was ready to make something out of nothing.

"Cops!" he shouted at the top of his lungs. Three men spun to face the light. Two raised their guns. Hannibal spun and charged for the trees. He could hear Cindy's footsteps to his left and slightly behind him.

In his mind the scene played out like a film in slow motion. Three men faced what they assumed was a threat. One second: looking for a target. Two seconds: focus on the car moving past them, looking hard to see if it bore the lights or lettering of an official vehicle. Three seconds: looking at each other, realizing they had been fooled. Four seconds: turning back, guns raised, staring into the darkness, wanting to kill their captives but not to fire shots that might get neighbors' attention unless they were sure they would hit their targets.

By then Hannibal and Cindy were thirty yards away and opening the gap with every step. That was a long shot with a handgun even in daylight with a stationary target. After a full five seconds the brothers finally decided to give chase. By then, Hannibal was past the first trees and into the wooded area.

"Left," he whispered to Cindy. Two steps later he said, "Down," and dropped into the dead leaves and moss. On his belly on the damp, cold ground he held as still as possible. Beside him, Cindy did the same. He leaned to get his mouth as close to her ear as possible.

"Do you still have your heels on?"

She nodded, still panting but as quietly as she could.

"Throw one. To the right. Hard as you can."

Hannibal tried to relax into the shadows. Cindy's clothes rustled. She gave a short grunt. After two seconds of silence he heard the desired crash through the trees, followed by three sets of footsteps. A simple deception, but he was betting that his pursuers had never gone camping or hiking.

"You okay?" he whispered.

"Just scared to death. What do we do?"

"First, can you get a tear going in this tape around my hands?
"

Cindy gave no verbal response but he heard her squirming around and then felt her breath on his arms. Her teeth did the job and once the duct tape was torn he was able to rip it and free his hands with little effort.

"Now?" she asked.

"Nearest house." Hannibal got to his feet with as little noise as possible. He kissed Cindy's cheek, then moved in a quiet crouch toward the back of the house on the right of George Washington Monroe's death site. First they stepped past the tree line onto the well-tended grass. Then Hannibal led his woman along the tree line until they stood facing the neighbor's sprawling deck. He dropped to his knees, she followed suit, and they moved toward the gate at a fast crawl.

By the time they reached the wooden steps Hannibal's knees were soaked and he figured Cindy's knees were sore. She must have regretted wearing a dress, but he was very glad they both wore black. Even if the Thomas brothers spotted their movement they would be darned difficult targets.

Were they in fact the Thomas brothers? Even as he crept up onto the hardwood deck, Hannibal wondered if the boys with different fathers had all taken their mother's name.

Cindy crawled up onto the deck and stopped beside Hannibal, leaning against the sliding glass door. Automatic lights glowed in the floor of the deck, but a large gas grill shielded her from outside eyes. For a moment they seemed safe. Hannibal jiggled the door handle.

"You going to knock?"

"I doubt I'd be heard," Hannibal said. "There are no lights on the main level. They're either downstairs in the media room taking in a movie, or upstairs in bed early. Either way, they wouldn't hear a knock on the back door."

"Can you force the door?"

"Maybe, but I'd rather break the glass." Hannibal glanced around the deck, then decided to raise the grill lid just enough to grab a section of the heavy cooking grate.

"With a house this fine, won't they have an alarm?" Cindy asked.

"Sure hope so," Hannibal said. "A nice loud one, that's connected to one of those services that sends the cops running in nine point eight seconds. Believe me, I want to get caught breaking in here. The Three Stooges will scatter but we can always find them later, when they're not the only ones with guns."

Hannibal waved Cindy away. Holding the iron grate with both hands he raised it overhead and swung it down, slamming a corner into the glass. He was anticipating the scream of an earsplitting alarm. What he got was the muted crackle of safety glass being pierced.

Cindy smirked. "No alarm."

"I'm betting they've got one and are just too lazy to set it when they're home."

"They might be even lazier," Cindy said. "What if no one's home?"

"Well, nothing says we can't go inside and call the police the old fashioned way."

Grateful for his gloves, Hannibal reached into the hole and flipped the lever to unlock the glass door. He slid it open and stepped inside, waving Cindy behind him. Sliding it closed, he locked it again, mostly by habit. Then he went to the bottom of the steps to the second floor.

"Hello, upstairs. If you're armed please don't fire. We're being pursued by muggers but you're safe if you stay where you are. Just let me know you're there, and then call the police." Greeted by silence, Hannibal opened the door to the lower level and made the same announcement.

"Looks like we're alone," Cindy said. "And it's kind of spooky in here. Can I turn on a light?"

"Not a good idea," Hannibal said. He pulled a mini Maglite from his jacket pocket. "Let's just find the phone and call for help."

Cindy followed him as they explored the house. The layout of the main level was very open, but two rooms had doors and Hannibal looked in both. One was clearly used as an office. If there was a phone he would have expected to find it there.

"Not seeing a land line. Maybe they just have cell phones."

"Nothing weird about that," Cindy said. "I don't have a land line in my place. But we do have the computer. I'll just send a series of tweets and Facebook everyone I know. Somebody will have to be at the keyboard."

Cindy sat down and turned the computer on. It was up and ready in less than two minutes, but after a few tentative taps at the keys she dropped her hands.

"So much for that idea," she said. "Password protected."

"What? Who the hell puts a password on their computer at home?"

Cindy slowly raised her hand. "Pretty much everybody but you. So, on to the next house?"

"Maybe." Hannibal went to the dining room window and eased the curtain back. He saw Eddie's bulky form lumber past. He had a gun now too.

"They're still wandering around out there," Hannibal said. "I think it's safer to stay here and make this place our fortress."

"For how long?"

"Well, when the owners come home we can get them to call the police," Hannibal said. "That's the safest option."

"With our luck they'll be out of town."

"In which case we'll leave in the morning," Hannibal said. "I doubt those three will roam the neighborhood all night. Even if they do, morning will bring safety. They're not going to gun us down in broad daylight."

With Hannibal in the lead they explored the lower level of the house, still partly hoping in vain for a telephone or unsecured computer. He also hoped the residents were hunters but there was no sign of any firearms, just fishing equipment in the storage room. He also found some basic tools and thought a hammer might be a handy last-ditch weapon, so he stuffed one into his belt.

The rest of the lower level was one big room the owners must have used for entertaining, with a guest room setup at one end and an exercise space at the other. It would be a safe place to hole up, but offered little concealment and only one door easily blocked. Besides, Hannibal wanted to be able to see outside so they moved back up. He detoured to the kitchen in search of a snack. After gathering cheese, crackers and a couple of sodas he turned to go and noticed Cindy leaning on the island with both hands.

"Tired, babe?"

"Exhausted. I'm sure it's more emotional than physical. Burned a lot of nervous energy."

Hannibal threw an arm around her. "Actually, you're doing really well. A lot of people just collapse after having a gun pointed at them. Once we're upstairs you can collapse. Can you take some of this stuff?"

Cindy took the two soda bottles. Hannibal reached to the professional looking knife block and slid out the biggest blade, a cleaver. Just in case.

"Hey, don't I get one?"

"Are you expecting to stab somebody?"

"No," Cindy said with a smile, "but I never expect to stab somebody." Hannibal nodded, and pulled out the second biggest knife as well.

Upstairs Hannibal looked into each room, making sure no Goldilocks was sleeping unaware of their presence. After some consideration he decided to bypass the cavernous master bedroom and settle in the second biggest of the four available. The room was decorated in muted pastels, as generic as any hotel room. In fact, he would have sworn the pictures on the wall were stolen from a hotel. Night tables on either side of the queen size bed held silver lamps. A dresser with a big mirror stood against the outside wall. He went in, dumped his food and weapons on the bed, then went back out and turned to face into the room.

Standing in the doorway he faced a window in the opposite wall. There were two windows in that wall, with the dresser between them. If he was oriented right, that was the east wall. They would get early morning sun. The wall to his right, the south wall, held a closet and the wall-mounted television. The door was at one end of the west wall. The head of the bed was pushed against the north wall. One could roll off the side of the bed to the east and hide from someone in the doorway.

"Relax here for a minute, babe," Hannibal said. "I've got an idea. Got to run downstairs but be right back."

Hannibal jogged down to the basement but on his way back up again stopped in the kitchen. He found a nice bottle of white wine chilling in the refrigerator and grabbed two glasses from the china cabinet and found a corkscrew in a kitchen drawer.

When he got back to his chosen room for the night he found Cindy propped up on two pillows on the bed just sitting in the dark. One of the kitchen knives was clutched tightly in her right fist.

"You okay?"

"Yeah. Didn't know if it was safe to turn on the TV."

"Probably wouldn't hurt anything," Hannibal said. "It certainly wouldn't make this house stand out from any of the others. Here, I thought this might be better than sodas. Why don't you pour us a couple glasses of wine while I fix up the door?"

While Cindy wrestled with the cork Hannibal hammered a nail into the edge of the bedroom door about four inches from the floor. Then he drove another nail into the doorsill at the same height. When he opened the door all the way it hit a doorstop on the south wall. Bracing the door with a foot, Hannibal tied a piece of fishing line to one nail then wound it tightly around the other. After four loops he cut it and tied it off. Just as Cindy was turning the television to an all music channel playing smooth jazz, Hannibal pushed the door almost closed. She was smiling as he joined her on the nice, firm mattress.

"And what was all that about?" she asked, handing him a glass.

"Just in case stuff," Hannibal replied. "Where's the cheese?"

"Right here next to me, but you didn't bring a plate or anything."

Hannibal glanced around for a substitute tray. After a moment of thought he pulled the drawer out of the table on his side of the bed. He flipped it over, sat it on the bed between them, and began to slice the bricks of sharp cheddar and Monterey jack with the knife he brought from the kitchen.

"If these people come home tonight they'll want to kill us."

"And if they don't we'll have to leave them some money for the use of their house, not to mention the destruction," Cindy said. Her voice was light, the way Hannibal remembered it before that day in Rockland's when she interrupted their lunch with a suicide attempt. She opened a sleeve of crackers and put it on their improvised tray. "Now, what's the just in case scenario?"

Hannibal bit into a cracker and held his answer for a second while his tongue smiled. It was a common saltine cracker but the sharp cheddar was exquisite, with just the right amount of bite. He chewed slowly, letting the flavor melt around the entire space of his mouth. And the wine was a perfect match, a Riesling he had never heard of with a flowery, almost perfumed, aroma.

"Well I was gaming in my mind, what if the three Stooges find us here? They might spot the broken window and decide to come in and look around. I didn't want to be surprised. I figure that improvised trip wire will slow down anyone popping into the room."

"You're planning for that?" Cindy asked.

"Of course. Here's the deal. If we hear someone in the house you hop over there and get in that closet. I roll off the bed over on this side. If I duck down I'm invisible from the door, but I can see whoever's coming in, in the mirror on the bureau."

Cindy emptied her wine glass and refilled it. "Won't he see you in the mirror too?"

"Not right away, babe. His eyes would go to the bed first. Anyway, when he pushes the door open the fishing line goes taut and becomes a trip wire. He goes down, I pop up and land on him. Threat neutralized."

"You, Mr. Jones, are too smart by half."

She turned to him and offered a smile that he recognized, one that he hadn't seen in a few days. How odd that in these peculiar circumstances she was not just happy but relaxed, he might even say content. He wasn't just looking at the woman he loved. This was the woman he fell in love with.

Hannibal leaned back against the pillows and let the day fall off him. They were safe, it was quiet, and the last few hours had burned off his energy. As he took a deep breath Cindy tipped to the side, leaning into him, her head rolling against his chest. His arm fell around her, holding her close. She giggled.

"You know, this is kind of romantic. Is that weird?"

"I no longer think I can spot weird when I see it."

"Would it be wrong to get freaky on a stranger's bed without them even knowing we're here?"

Hannibal smiled and leaned up to gather the cheese and crackers back onto his improvised tray. "Nothing's wrong if you don't get caught, right? But we don't want to make a mess…"

"Yes I do," Cindy said, nipping at his ear with her teeth and starting to work the buttons of his shirt. "I want to get real messy."

## -18-

Sometimes sleep is a gift the universe offers you. Other days you have to reach out and grab it for yourself. Sleep had come easily to Hannibal after the final release, but now he was having a hard time holding onto it.

He had been all tangled up with Cindy's soft, warm body. The sound of her breathing, deep and tender as her heart slowed, was a lullaby to him. But now something was trying to force him back into the world. He resisted. This was paradise, huddled in the darkness in a cocoon of love, breathing the scent of her hair, feeling her arms around him. He didn't want to wake up. If he did he might lose this effortless joy. If not for that stupid noise...

His eyes popped open. The sound was slow, but nonetheless rhythmic like a dripping faucet. Those were footsteps. Someone was walking but very slowly. Someone was in the house.

Hannibal's pulse rate tripled as reality rushed in on him. He pulled his head away from Cindy's gentle half-snore, not reacting when she cuddled in closer to him. The footsteps stopped, then picked up their regular beat again.

So someone was in the house. The owners? Unlikely. If they didn't know they had intruders they would move normally and make a lot more noise. Police? Even less likely. They would have announced themselves loudly just for safety's sake and to give any intruders a chance to show themselves without risking being shot. Putting aside the unlikely coincidence of an actual burglary, Hannibal knew one of the three brothers was searching the house for them.

The darkness was not as deep as when Hannibal had fallen asleep. Dawn was only minutes, maybe seconds away. Had those idiots searched the neighborhood for them all night? Had one of them finally spotted the broken sliding glass door? Had they found the trail Hannibal and Cindy left when they crawled across the yard to the deck? That string of suppositions seemed outrageous, but nothing else made sense. And there they lay, naked under rumpled sheets.

"Hey, babe," he whispered. Cindy stirred but clung to sleep as he had. "Cindy. Sweetheart. You need to wake up now. We've got company."

Her eyes lagged behind her smile, snapping open a second after her lips moved into a frown. She looked into Hannibal's eyes to see how bad things were. He watched her expression pass through confusion to fear and then to that face that was an unvoiced question.

"Not to worry," he whispered. "I got this. But I want you to go stand in the closet so you don't get caught up in it if shit gets serious."

Cindy considered only for a second before nodding and rolling away from him. She made no sound lowering one foot to the floor, then easing herself upright. She was standing on her dress. She looked at her panties and blew a puff of derisive air at her absurd situation. She snatched up her red lace bra and the knife she brought from the kitchen and tiptoed to the closet.

Hannibal maintained his easy smile until Cindy closed the closet door. Then he pushed off the sheet and grabbed his pants from the floor on his side of the bed. He listened closely to the distant footsteps, feeling the timing. He timed his own feet hitting the floor with those distant steps, then quickly pulled on his pants. They were dirty, and the knees were still wet but he'd just have to deal with it. He knew the situation could turn violent and there was no way he was going to get into a tussle with another man naked.

Crouching between the bed and the dresser he went back over the events of the day, trying to understand how he had come to this place. So many misunderstanding, so much confusion and misdirection had led to this moment when a man he didn't even know twenty-four hours before would try to kill him. And he may be forced to return the favor.

The unknown footsteps moved up the stairs. This was a cautious man, whose steps implied that he was looking around every corner before moving forward. Not Eddie then. He'd be more the bull in the china shop. Probably not Nas. He would go for help rather than explore the house alone. This would be Darryl. Darryl, the driver, the planner. He would have stationed his brothers at the front and back door while he came in to settle things.

Outside the room, Hannibal heard the explorer go to the master bedroom door. A pause. Shove it open. Stillness. Step to the second bedroom. Repeat the process.

Hannibal's hand was wet on the knife's handle. He tightened his grip as the enemy came to his room door. This would be it. If the man was armed Hannibal would have to kill him. He might never really know why this man had forced his own murder. That bothered Hannibal more than he wanted to think. His woman would see it happen. That bothered him more.

The steps stopped just outside the door. Hannibal tensed, teeth clenched, knife held tightly, tip forward.

The first weak rays of dawn sliced through the windows. Darryl shoved the door open. He held the pistol with the silencer with both hands, aimed at what had been Hannibal's pillow. Hannibal stood, braced to leap forward.

And Darryl took one long step forward, stepping right over the taut wire attached to the bottom of the door. His barrel swung to target Hannibal's bare chest, its muzzle only a dozen feet away from Hannibal's heart.

Yep, Hannibal thought. Shit just got real.

The two men stood poised just long enough for Hannibal to take one breath and for Darryl to start a smile.

Hannibal lowered his shoulders trying to look less threatening. "You don't look like a killer to me, Darryl. This is not the time to do something you will regret later."

"Oh, I ain't going to regret killing you, you murderous son of a bitch."

A lot can happen in one second.

Hannibal stepped to the left, pivoting his body so that its left edge faced Darryl, becoming as small a target as possible. Even at this distance the gunman could miss, and Hannibal was confident that he could close the gap and get his knife into the man before he could fire again.

Darryl began squeezing his trigger, adjusting his aim and looking down the sights with grim determination.

Both men froze as a terrorized scream filled the room and Cindy burst from the closet, diving forward, clutching her knife with both hands over her head.

Darryl spun toward her but she was already dropping. He was farther away than she realized. Her knees thudded onto the floor. Darryl's gun swung over her head as her arms drove the knife down, not into his heart but into his thigh just above his right knee. Darryl's scream picked up where Cindy's had left off.

At the end of that crucial second Hannibal left hand clamped around Darryl's right wrist, pointing the pistol toward the ceiling. His right fist crashed across Darryl's jaw. Darryl's head thumped into the door behind him and he slid to the floor, unconscious.

A voice filled with hate shouted Darryl's name from downstairs. Hannibal grabbed the gun and dropped to the floor. He lay with his head and shoulders in the hall, arms outstretched toward the stairs. His legs were over Darryl's. He felt his left calf pressed against the knife in Darryl's leg and quickly pulled it away.

Two pairs of feet pounded up the stairs. Eddie came into view first carrying the big magnum. As he turned toward Hannibal, Hannibal fired. It wouldn't be heard outside the house but it was loud enough. The bullet punched the middle of Eddie's chest, throwing him back against the wall. Behind him, Nas pointed Hannibal's own gun in the general direction of the source of the shot, but his eyes flicked back at Eddie.

"Put the gun down," Hannibal said, using the command voice he had learned as a New York City cop. "Right now!" Silently he thought, *I'm a small target down here on the floor half behind a wall. You're fully exposed. Do the smart thing. Please.*

Nas' hand began to shake. He took three quick breaths, as if trying to build up his courage. But then he slowly lowered the gun to the floor.

"Thank you," Hannibal said, keeping his gun trained on the last man standing. "I didn't want things to go this way."

Nas nodded. "My brothers," he said. It was as much a question as a statement. Hannibal nodded back.

"Do you have a phone?" When Nas nodded, Hannibal said, "Call 9-1-1. If they can get an ambulance here fast enough, maybe nobody dies today."

## -19-

"You look like hell," Orson Rissik said.

"That's just because you've never seen me without my glasses," Hannibal replied. He was sitting on the porch steps of the brick front colonial in which he had spent the night, elbows resting on his knees, his hands hanging between.

Looking up at Rissik's passive face Hannibal knew his friend was right. His suit was a soiled, grass-stained mess. His shoes were scuffed and caked with mud. And there was a nasty bruise on his cheek thanks to Eddie's knuckles the night before.

The morning sun glared over Rissik's shoulder when he stepped aside to allow a stretcher to pass. Both men watched Darryl being loaded into the back of an ambulance.

"That's why so many people don't get you," Rissik said. His gray suit was cut sharp as a razor, as always. He made Hannibal long for a shower and a change of clothes.

"Am I supposed to know what you're talking about?"

"Maybe not," Rissik said. "Maybe that's why I like you. What I meant was, a lot of people who heard the story of last night wouldn't get why you would put a tourniquet on that boy's leg and keep him alive until the paramedics got here. He'd have killed you as easy as breathing."

Cindy came out of the house wrapped in a blanket. She stood behind her man and rested a hand on his head. "That's kind of what makes him Hannibal, don't you think?"

When the police and emergency personnel arrived she had declared that she couldn't force herself back into her dress. She had sat wrapped in the blanket while they took her statement. Hannibal had given his in a different room. There were endless questions and the truth was a bit complicated but he was patient with the young officers. He knew they were just doing their job but he was a lot more comfortable when Rissik arrived. After that, the conversation could be a little less one-sided.

"I'm glad my efforts weren't wasted. How's Eddie?"

"The big guy?" Rissik asked. "That's one tough son of a bitch. The docs said he'll be good as new in a week or two."

"And Nas?"

"Didn't resist when we took him into custody," Rissik said. "He begged me to let him call his mother. I told the boys to let him call from the car on the way to the detention center. That must have been an interesting conversation."

Hannibal chuckled. "You have no idea. I met their mother. He's probably glad he's going to be in a cell where he's safe from her." He stood up slowly, glancing over at the remains of the house that came so close to being his unmarked grave.

"So you know these guys?"

"Sort of," Hannibal said.

"I figured they were just three of the hundreds of thugs you've pissed off in the last few years. At least, that's what I figured until I realized where we are. That's Wash Monroe's place you're staring at, isn't it? This all has something to do with his murder. Between that and this crap, property values here are going to go to hell."

Hannibal offered a half smile. That was probably as close to a joke as Rissik would ever get.

"Speaking of which, where the hell are the owners of this house?" Cindy asked. "I keep thinking of them driving up and seeing all these police cars and an ambulance pulling away from their house."

"Not even an issue," Rissik said. "The neighbors tell us they're in Europe on vacation for another week. If they knew what happened in their house, they'd probably extend their vacation."

Hannibal squinted against the morning sun, missing his sunglasses but knowing he would never find them out there in the yard. He assumed they would eventually get eaten by a lawn mower. "When they get back they're going to want to know everything that happened to their home. Sure hope I'm not the one who's going to have to explain it to them."

"Don't know about that," Rissik said, "But you're sure as hell going to have to explain it all to me."

"Orson, do you suppose we could save the official statements until after we get to some fresh clothes?"

Rissik huffed out a sigh. "I suppose the statements can wait until tomorrow. I'll be occupied questioning your assailants, even though they look more like the victims. Just tell me if you think they had anything to do with Monroe's murder."

Hannibal chuckled. "Best I could gather, they think it was me. They came after me to avenge his death. But I've got one wild idea who the killer might be. I don't think I can confirm it on my own, but if you could do a little digging into some government records for me…"

"Why of course Mister Detective Man, of course I'll do your research and legwork for you," Rissik said, slapping Hannibal's back. "Is there anything else I can do for you? A massage perhaps?"

"Well, actually, do you suppose we could get a ride back to Crystal City? That's where I left my car before these nitwits snatched us up."

A crisp fall breeze cut into Hannibal as he stepped out of Rissik's car. Crystal City was a whole different place in the light of day. Being the commercial side of Arlington, traffic was dense on a Monday morning. The river of cars was slow but the tide was strong, the flow forcing its way down Route 1 toward the Pentagon or on into The District. Tributaries branched off to flow down into the underground parking lots. And Hannibal knew there was even more hustle and bustle underground where a mass of commuters poured out of the Metro trains into rented government space. Those offices filled the buildings on the east side of Route 1, AKA Richmond Highway, AKA Jefferson Davis Highway.

There wasn't that much foot traffic, but the people who were on the street all walked like they had someplace to be and were already late. Hannibal had to force his way into that flow to open the front passenger door for Cindy. She thanked Rissik for the ride, turned to take Hannibal's outstretched hand, and stood as close to him as possible. As the car pulled away Hannibal looked down into her face, scrubbed clean and fresh. He loved her without makeup and with her hair just a little unruly.

"You are lovely."

Her head fell forward into his chest. "Get me into your car."

"Self-conscious?"

"Hannibal, I'm standing on the street wrapped in a…"

"Mr. Jones!" A voice called from behind him. Cindy pulled even closer to him, muttering, "Oh, no," under her breath.

Hannibal turned to see the woman pushing through the crowd rushing to work, shoved downstream a bit but pushing back up to meet them at the curb.

"Mrs. Thomas, what are you doing here?" Hannibal asked. He had imagined her a night person and expected her to sleep until noon. She wore casual clothes this time, black slacks with a plain white blouse and tennis shoes, but her hair and makeup were perfect. He felt Cindy cringe in self comparison.

"Mr. Jones I had to see you, to apologize," Sarah Thomas said. "Nasir called me, woke me up to tell me where he was and more important, what he had done. After I got finished cussing him out I knew I had to talk to you. I figured you'd have to come back for your car so I waited and…"

The rush of Sarah's words had taken Hannibal by surprise and frozen him in place. Now she paused, as if seeing them for the first time. Her mouth stayed open as she took in Cindy's appearance. A revolving series of emotions played across her face: guilt, pity, sorrow, confusion, and back to guilt. Her right hand reached out but didn't quite touch Cindy's shoulder.

"Oh my Lord, you poor child. You have had a horrible night and here I am running on and, well I know you have NEVER appeared in public looking like that. You must be… please,

please come down in my office. We need to get you cleaned up, and I think I have some things in your size."

Sarah stepped back and directly into a marching businessman. He thumped into her, scowled, but then was swept away by the human current. Hannibal wrapped an arm around Cindy's shoulders and guided her across the sidewalk. Sarah opened the door to The Lucent and waved them inside. Clearly she had been expecting them, since the door was already unlocked.

Without patrons or workers, the place reminded Hannibal of a movie set. There was a sense that this place was not quite real. A faint scent of pine hung in the air and everything gleamed, even the poles. Sarah guided them to the elevator, followed only by the echo of their footsteps on the tile.

The ride down was short and a bit claustrophobic. Hannibal was braced for action when the doors slid open but of course they faced nothing but an empty room. Sarah quickly ushered Cindy out and across her office to an almost hidden door. Hannibal stood for a moment, surprised to be left alone. When he heard a shower running he sat in the same chair he had used on his last visit. He followed his girl's unseen actions by sound alone while replaying his last conversation in that room.

The flowing water ended. Soft footsteps. Hangers scraped across a rod. Material ruffled. Muted conversation. A quiet giggle that could only be his girl. Hannibal smiled. And as he listened he mentally sorted through the clues Sarah had shared when they talked.

When the two women reappeared Cindy was transformed. The simple, bright blue sleeveless dress fit her as if it were made for her. The wide belt accented her trim waist. Her hair had been curled and brushed out to give it life without calling attention to itself. Her face, her arms, her legs, all of her skin glowed with freshness. That, the lack of jewelry, and the fact that she was barefoot made her seem years younger to Hannibal. This was the Cindy Santiago he might have met in High School.

"What are you staring at lover?" Cindy asked. Hannibal just smiled, and after a moment, Cindy giggled a bit. Like a schoolgirl.

"Come over here, honey," Sarah said. "Let's finish off that look." She guided Cindy to a vanity with a three-part mirror. She sat Cindy facing the mirrors and began to work her hair with a brush and short spurts of hairspray.

"I've got a feeling you wish The Lord had sent you a little girl," Hannibal said.

"That's why I kept trying," Sarah said, smiling at him in the mirror. "But you know I love my boys, every one of them."

"I'm sure of it. That's why I was going to visit you later today anyway. I think you'd do just about anything to help Darryl, Eddie and Nas out of the trouble they've gotten themselves in."

Sarah moved the brush a little more slowly. "Look I know they did wrong but I was hoping we could find a way to get past this business. They didn't really hurt you…"

Hannibal waved her words away. "Last night is small stuff. I don't intend to press any charges if that's what you're worrying about."

"I knew you were a right guy."

"But that's just the tip of the iceberg," Hannibal said. "Your boys are implicated in a couple of murders."

Sarah's face clouded up. "You think my boys really killed somebody?"

"I don't know. I don't think so. They made it clear to me that they really cared about Wash, so it's hard for me to imagine them hurting him. But the court might not see it the way I do."

"What can I do?" Sarah asked. Cindy's hair was almost perfectly styled as Sarah's expert hands moved of their own accord. "There must be something… some way I can help my boys."

"Actually, there is something." Hannibal locked eyes with Sarah in the mirror. "If you will help me get access to some official records, I think I can figure this all out and maybe keep Darryl and Eddie and Nas from facing a life sentence."

## -20-

Hannibal grinned, and then admitted to himself that the oddest things would make him smile. In this case he was thinking about government euphemisms. People passed away instead of dying. Fanatics didn't commit genocide but instead engaged in ethnic cleansing. Women had pregnancy terminations instead of abortions. And Fairfax County, Virginia didn't have a jail. No, they had an Adult Detention Center.

Hannibal got as comfortable as he could in a purposely uncomfortable chair in the visiting area of that Center, which was almost within shouting distance of Rissik's office. The stark gray blocks of the jail sat right next door to the imposing brick county courthouse building with its trio of three-story arches on the front. County police offices also shared the grounds of the Public Safety Center – whose name gave Hannibal another smile.

While he waited Hannibal stared at the blank, beige wall of the visitors' area, replaying the week's events like an old, sepia-toned movie. A week had passed since his visit with Sarah, and it had been a challenging week for him and Cindy. Monday she had returned to work, playing catch-up on the cases she was working before her world had collapsed. Hannibal had a mountain of correspondence he had ignored, but while he tended to it he continued to dig into the dark corners of the life of George Washington Monroe. He was sure that was the path to understanding his death.

A deputy swung the door open and Hannibal stayed quiet as Darryl limped into the room. It saddened Hannibal to see how natural Darryl looked in a bright orange jumpsuit. The prisoner settled into the chair across the table and glared at his visitor.

"Thanks for seeing me," Hannibal said.

"Wanted to see mama."

"Of course," Hannibal said. "She's talking with Nas right now. And I know Sarah told you to let me talk to you." He also knew she was taking care of her boys. Darryl was clean shaven, his hair was brushed and Hannibal could smell a very masculine cologne. Personal hygiene was one way an inmate could hang onto his humanity when surrounded by animals.

"Yeah." Darryl almost spit the word. "Now I got to wait a week to see her. One visitor a week. You better have something mighty damn worthy to say to show why it ought to be you."

"I do. Unless you like the idea of being stuck in here. Is this your idea of a nice vacation?"

"Very funny," Darryl said. "I hate this place."

"Yeah, you and thirteen hundred other knuckleheads. Except maybe you don't deserve to be here."

To his credit, Darryl stared straight into Hannibal's eyes. "No, man. We did what we did. Kidnapping is what it was, and I'll take the rap for what I did. But it was me, alright? I forced Eddie and Nas into it."

Hannibal brushed the lie out of the air with his hand. "What you did to me, that's not even the point, man."

"So what is the point?" Darryl leaned in, the edge of his hands slapping the table.

"The point?" Hannibal repeated through clenched teeth. "The point is the woman. The woman who was gunned down right in front of me. I can't just let that go."

"So?"

"So? You do realize I've got enough on you to pin that murder to you, don't you?"

Hannibal figured Darryl must play a lot of poker. He closed his eyes for half a second, but betrayed no concern. He just said, "Maybe."

Hannibal was a poker player too, and knew how to play a weak hand. "No maybe about it, moron. I can make sure you go down for this."

"That's bullshit," Darryl said, leaning back. "I ain't kill nobody."

"I don't think you did," Hannibal said in a quieter tone. "but I think you can help me figure out who did."

A new light appeared in Darryl's eyes, a light he rushed to hide. "No, I don't think I can."

"Don't think you can, or don't think you will?"

"No, I can't," Darryl said, shaking his head. "I just can't. And even if I could, why the hell would I want to help you? Your bitch stabbed me in the leg."

Hannibal looked down and took a breath. When he looked up he bared his teeth. "You don't disrespect her."

"She shouldn't have stabbed me."

"You shouldn't have pointed a gun at me."

"You shouldn't have killed Papa Wash."

Hannibal rolled his eyes to the ceiling. "Jesus, you're an idiot. Look, you want to see your mama today or not?"

"Sure I do, but so what?" Darryl asked. "You ain't no cop. You ain't nobody. You ain't got the juice to get me allowed a second visitor today."

"No," Hannibal said, "But I know somebody who's got the juice to take you out of here for a couple hours. Now what do you say?"

## -21-

"I don't know, Hannibal," Cindy said, massaging his shoulders. "Do you really think this will work? I mean, it made sense when you laid it out for me this morning, but…"

Sitting in his desk chair Hannibal reached up to cover her hands with his own. "What you're really asking me is, can I read people. That's what it comes down to, babe. If he's the man I think he is, it will work."

"I should just go with you," she said, bending to speak into his ear. "Things may not go as planned."

"That's exactly why you shouldn't go with me," Hannibal said. "When the time comes, I'll need my officer-of-the-court type witness in a safe, neutral corner."

A solid knock on Hannibal's office door interrupted her. Orson Rissik called, "Are we going to do this or not?"

The Lucent was hopping when Hannibal arrived. The music was louder than it was on his previous visit, and nearly twice as many people packed the tables. He thought the lights were lower but it could have been the effect of the deeper crowd. The bar was three deep and the girls slipped through the crowd like quick, slender fish to serve the tables. He stood at the door for a moment, taking in the atmosphere and tapping his foot to the go-go beat that was driving the dancers' hips around their poles. Then one of the curvy servers, a tall brunette, spotted him and rerouted her path to cruise past the door.

"Good evening, Tahnee," Hannibal said. "Nice to see you again."

Her face reflected surprise that he remembered her name. Tahnee winked and smiled, but kept moving. "Table twelve. Front left."

She moved on across the floor with Hannibal barely able to keep her in sight. He managed to avoid bumping into anyone despite the fact that most of the men on their feet were watching the stage, not where they were going. When he came within sight of his target he slowed and let Tahnee continue on her rounds. He took a couple of deep breaths, watching his quarry sip cognac.

Show time.

Hannibal walked past the table, spun, and dropped into the chair facing Kevin Larson.

"What's up, Kevin?"

Kevin was dressed for Saturday night: inexpensive but well-fitted chocolate suit and alligator shoes. His eyes stayed on the show over Hannibal's shoulder for a second before he recognized that he had company."

"Mister Jones. How you doing this evening? Didn't expect to see you here."

"I've been here once or twice before," Hannibal said. He wondered where his wife thought he was. "This a regular stop for you?"

"Time to time," Kevin said, sipping his drink. Hannibal knew he had been invited there this particular night to meet someone.

"I do like this place," Hannibal said, "but tonight I'm not here to watch the girls work the pole. I'm here to see you."

Kevin blinked and Hannibal caught a glimpse of a cleverness he had not noticed in those eyes before. It vanished as quickly as it appeared. "I don't get it. Why would you come looking for me?"

"I wanted to talk a little more about Wash and his poor wife. About how they came to be dead."

"Uh-huh. How'd you find me, anyway?"

Hannibal shrugged. "I'm a detective."

"Yeah, you said. And I guess you must be pretty good at it." Kevin looked around himself as if he imagined spies in every corner. Hannibal leaned in a little closer.

"Damn straight, bud. But it don't pay as good as you might think. That's why I want to talk to you about the whole Wash thing."

Kevin put the edges of his hands on the table in the universal sign for openness. "Look, I'm a simple man. You're going to have to be a lot clearer than that."

"I will," Hannibal said, standing. "But not here. At least not out here in the open."

"Well I'm not going anywhere with you."

"Chill, man," Hannibal said. "I've got a deal here with the management." Hannibal raised his hand and gave a small wave. In seconds Tahnee was beside the table. Hannibal waved her closer, handed her a wad of bills and spoke in low tones.

"I need a room with some privacy," he said. "No girls, just a space for a little meeting."

Tahnee nodded, thought for a second, and waved to Hannibal to follow her. As she walked away, Hannibal stood and motioned with his head for Kevin to join them.

"And why should I go anywhere with you?" Kevin asked, leaning back.

Hannibal rested both palms on the table and leaned in. "Because, trust me, your life will turn to shit if you don't." Then he turned and walked toward the stage, keeping Tahnee's shapely behind in sight. At the very front of the room he turned left and looked back. Kevin was following at a discreet distance, looking puzzled and trying hard to hide his still significant limp.

Tahnee led them through a door and down a short hall. She stopped at a door and produced a key from someplace and unlocked it. Then she continued down the hall. Hannibal stepped into the room and left the door standing open. Kevin followed, closing the door behind himself.

The space was plain with dull gray walls and a wooden floor. Four comfortable looking chairs faced each other with plenty of space between them and a small table beside each one. Lighting was dim, but not so low one could overlook the four-poster bed at the far end. It wasn't quite a separate room, but partial walls a couple of feet wide on either side gave the bed its own little alcove. Close-set strings of beads hung to the floor across the wide central opening. Hannibal guessed this was the place for very private lap dances with an option for more. He settled into a chair. The table beside it held a bottle of Hennessy and a pair of glasses.

"I observed that you are a cognac man, right?"

Kevin stayed by the door. "All right, I'm here. So what's this all about?"

"I figured you must have an idea," Hannibal said, opening the bottle, "or you wouldn't have come. Have a seat."

"Well, you said it had to do with Wash's death," Kevin said, easing himself into the chair facing Hannibal.

"That's the topic all right," Hannibal said. "He's gone, his wife is gone, and I figure you're in for one hell of an inheritance. To put it simply, I want my share."

For the next ten seconds the only sound in the room was the gurgle and splash of Hannibal pouring each glass almost full. He wondered if he hadn't been pouring if he might have heard the gears turning in Kevin's head. Kevin was used to hiding behind a screen of pretended simple-mindedness. Hannibal wondered how he would play it this time.

When Kevin again met Hannibal's gaze he said, "What are you saying? Did Wash leave a will? I was just his personal assistant but he didn't really have anyone else so I suppose it's possible…"

"Don't try to shine me on," Hannibal said, holding a glass out to Kevin. "We both know Wash didn't have time to change his will after his wife was killed. You get the money because you're his only heir. His loving son."

Kevin's eyes got wild for a moment. He sat straighter. He glanced at the door and for a second Hannibal thought he had misjudged the man. But then he relaxed, turned to squarely face Hannibal, and accepted his glass.

"What in the world would make you think such a thing?"

Hannibal sipped his drink and smiled. "You know, it's funny what a guy will overlook. Three guys tried to kill me last week. They were Sarah's boys. When they came after me I had the feeling they were sent by somebody else. I mean, Darryl's got the street smarts but he's not a leader, or a mastermind. And there was no reason for him to think I killed Wash, unless somebody told him so. Somebody he trusted. Then I remembered that Sarah told us she had four sons. It made sense that the oldest boy would be the ring leader, hiding in the shadows."

"Makes sense, I guess," Kevin said, trying on his confused face again, "but how does that connect to Wash?"

"Well, Sarah told me she got married twice," Hannibal said, taking another sip and letting the smooth warmth spread through him. "She had three kids by two husbands, and no more after. So even though she didn't say so, I figured son number four must have been the first. And he had to be by Wash."

"Really? He never said anything to me about having a son. He ever talk about having kids to you?"

Hannibal shook his head. "No, that wasn't his path. He needed to be unencumbered. I figure he effectively disowned his son, and his sorta stepsons, when he paid Sarah off to get out of his life."

Kevin screwed his face up, then took a long drink from his glass. "You saying he had a son he never acknowledged? What kind of brother does that?"

"The kind of brother that thinks he'll make more money with a pretty white wife and no past."

Kevin took his glass, stood up and started to slowly roam the room. "Wow, if my father did me like that…"

"Yeah, but he did," Hannibal said with a big smile. "All he ever gave you was that limp, and a job. Sarah told me she got him to give all her boys jobs."

"Naw, Jack. I worked for Wash all right, but Uncle Sam gave me this bum leg."

"Nice try, man. Your whole story hangs together as long as nobody suspects you, but it don't stand a close look. For example, Sarah told me Wash paid for surgery for one of her boys. I thought it might be for a club foot. The other three boys have nothing like that in their medical records. So, following my instincts I figured I'd check your medical records. With Sarah's permission and a police assist I'll have them in a few days. Not that I need them to prove you lied."

"I don't have to listen to this crap," Kevin said, moving in front of Hannibal and staring down at him. "I told you I picked up some shrapnel in this leg during a firefight."

"Yeah, you told me that," Hannibal said, standing to face him. "Right after you showed me all your pretty medals. Impressive stuff, and your only real mistake. I expect you earned all those medals..."

"Damn right I did!"

"Yeah, but there was one missing from the collection. No Purple Heart. My dad was Army, but that medal looks the same no matter what service you're in, and it's the one medal you would have to get if you were injured in combat."

"That don't prove nothing," Kevin mumbled.

"Guess not," Hannibal said, "but the lie and the fact that you changed your name is enough to get a warrant and force a DNA test. And you being Wash's son gives you a damn good motive to kill him. You wanted the fortune he spent a lifetime building."

"A fortune you want some of, I take it," Kevin said. He tipped his glass up, draining it, and dropped it back on the table. "Even if you were right, I don't see how a motive would be enough to make a man split his fair and just inheritance."

"Oh, no, I got the holy trifecta of investigations," Hannibal said. He held up his thumb. "Motive: the fact that you're his only heir." He raised his first finger. "Means: in your time with the Force Recon boys you sure had the chance to learn how to break a man's neck, and how to use a Molotov cocktail to burn down a house. The skills Wash's killer had." He added his middle finger. "Opportunity. As Wash's personal assistant, you had the pass codes to his security system so you could get in the house any time you wanted to. So tell me, did you drug his liquor? Or just wait until he got too drunk to move? I guess it don't matter. Refill?"

Kevin stared hard into the lenses of Hannibal's Oakleys. Hannibal smiled. Kevin nodded. Hannibal poured. Kevin sipped. "None of that proves I killed him. It's all circumstantial."

"I suppose." Hannibal leaned back, smiling bigger. "But my theory explains the only motive for Irene Monroe to be murdered. I don't know what kind of crap you told your accomplices, but we both know the only reason she needed to die was so you'd be Wash's only heir. And while I can't prove you murdered Wash, I got real evidence that you did Irene."

"That sounds like bullshit to me," Kevin said. He emptied his glass, slammed it on the table, and shoved his hands into his pockets.

That brought Hannibal to his feet. "You arrogant bastard. You gun her down right in front of my face and drive off and you think nothing happens? Didn't you think I'd catch the license, make and model of the car? Didn't you think I could trace that stolen car and find out who snatched it? And if they put you in a lineup, do you realize how easy it would be for me to lie and identify the guys in the car?"

Kevin gave one sharp laugh and pulled his hands out of his pockets. "That's what you got? That's what you got? Nigger I ain't giving you shit."

"What?" It was Hannibal's turn to put his glass down hard. He jumped to his feet, backing Kevin up. "You got to pay me. I got you dead to rights."

Kevin shook his head, grinning, and wagged a finger in Hannibal's face. "You talk like you street, and you acting like just another brother on the hustle, but you don't got no street sense, do you? Well, let me tell you how this plays out in a court room." Kevin walked as he talked, wandering behind his chair.

"So you identify everybody who was in the car and they drag us in. The police know every one of them pretty good. Me? I got no criminal record at all, man. Not even a parking ticket. I just point at my brothers and say they dragged me into all this. Gee, judge, it was all Darryl's idea. He's the leader of them boys. And he pulled the trigger on the white girl."

Hannibal lets a shadow of doubt pass across his face. "Is that true?"

"Don't matter," Kevin said. "The cops and the DA, they don't give a shit about the truth or justice. They care about conviction rates, and closing cases. They look at Darryl's record, all that assault and burglary and drug stuff, and the DA sees a slam dunk and looks right past me."

Kevin threw his head back to laugh, but his expression switched to shock when beads in the alcove rattled apart.

"You son of a bitch!" Darryl burst out of the darkness with hatred glowing in his eyes. "You ain't gonna put that on me!"

Kevin took a long step back, pulling a revolver out of his pocket. He pointed the gun at his brother's face for an instant, before Hannibal leaped forward to lock both hands around the gun. He then spun to his right, pulling Kevin by his outstretched right arm, angling the killer's face down into the back of the chair. Over his shoulder he saw two uniformed officers burst from the alcove behind Darryl, tackle him and pull him to the floor.

Orson Rissik strolled past that wrestling match toward the main event in the middle of the room. As Hannibal took the revolver, Rissik took control of Kevin, drawing his arms back to lock them in a pair of handcuffs. Only then did Cindy step out of the other room, keeping her distance from all the others. Kevin's eyes burned into Darryl's.

"What the hell are you doing here?"

"The better question is, why did your mother invite you here tonight, and provide me a room for my friends to wait for us in?"

"That was pretty ballsy, pal," Rissik said. "But I got to admit you played it mighty well. Remind me never to play poker with you."

"I'm just happy I got him to go where I needed him to go."

"You did that," Rissik said. "I don't think you could have ever gotten the other brothers to tell the truth if one of them didn't hear for themselves how ready this one was to throw them under the bus. But now…"

"Oh, hell yeah," Darryl said. The officers pulled him to his feet but held his arms, just in case. "You better believe it was all Kevin's idea. I'll cop to driving the car that night and take whatever I got coming to me, but Kevin took the shot. Nas will back me up on that. He was in the car with us."

"Okay, but why the hell kill poor Irene Monroe in the first place?" Rissik asked Darryl. "I mean, we know why he did it, but why did *you* think she had to die?"

Darryl paused and seemed to calm down. When he looked up he spoke to Hannibal instead of Rissik. "Look Jones… I'm real sorry for the way we done you. I swear Kevin had us all convinced that you was a hit man for hire. He said Irene was cheating on Wash, and she was planning to have him killed so she and her boy toy could run off with all his money."

"Shut up!" Kevin said, but Rissik slammed him down into the chair and held him down by his shoulders.

"Screw you, Kevin," Darryl said. "Look, we was watching her that night, planning to take her out. Then you showed up. Kevin said she was making the deal with you to kill Wash right then, and we had to stop that deal. And, honest to God, man, he had us all convinced that you killed Wash."

"Seriously?" Hannibal said. "You going to make it sound like this was a spontaneous decision? What about Irene's body? You guys came back and snatched her up, what, as a practical joke on the hired killer you thought I was?"

Kevin and Darryl locked eyes. It seemed clear that Kevin was done talking. Darryl took a deep breath and shook his head.

"That was Eddie," Darryl said. "He was hiding nearby. Kevin told him what to do to clean up the scene. He rolled the woman up in a plastic sheet and drove her away in her own car. I don't think I could have done that, but Eddie, he's got a pretty strong stomach."

"And Jason?" Cindy asked. When Darryl gave her a blank look she clenched her teeth and said, "Jason Moore. The boy toy, you called him. He was my friend. Why did he have to die?"

Darryl stared at the carpet in a way that made Hannibal smile. He actually looked embarrassed. "I'm sorry, ma'am. Me and the boys grabbed him. Kevin figured nobody would believe Irene was gunned down if there was no body, so the story would be that she ran off. But everybody knew she wouldn't run off by herself. Running off with her boyfriend, that sounded more believable. So he came up with the whole train story."

"Right," Rissik said. "You delivered this total stranger to your big brother, who grabbed his head and snapped his neck, like the Marine Recon boys taught him. I've had to deal with the Asian gangs from time to time but you boys are about the coldest I've seen."

"It wasn't like that," Darryl said. "We didn't know Kevin was going kill him until after it was done. It was a dirty business, but you got to understand, we'd do anything to protect Wash. He was so good to all of us." Darryl turned dagger eyes on Kevin.

"Nice story," Kevin said through a crooked smile. "But no jury's going to believe those three thugs over me. I'll still put it all on you, Darryl. You the brains here."

"No offense to Darryl," Hannibal said, "but that's a hell of a stretch. You think people will believe that your half-brothers killed three people, including the man who supported them all their lives, and cooked up this convoluted plot so you could inherit a fortune. Like Irene used to say, that would be like going all around your elbow to get to your asshole."

"I still can't believe it," Cindy said. She moved close enough to stare down into Kevin's eyes. "Not after meeting your people.

You're no street thug. And this man was no stranger to you. How could you kill your own father?"

Kevin sneered at her. "I ain't got to tell you shit."

"Then tell me." Sarah Thomas slipped through the door and walked up to her son. "How could you do all this? I didn't raise you to be a killer."

"You set me up," Kevin said, twisting around for a better view of his mother. "Inviting me down to see the show, to tell me what happened to my half-brothers, like I didn't know. You had this room all set up for them to con me, bad as Wash used to con his marks."

"Yes, I learned something from watching Wash's pyramid plan deceptions," Sarah said, "and when Mr. Jones here told me what he suspected, well, I had to hear it for myself. It broke my heart to see what you have become, son. And I still need for you to tell me how you could kill the man who brought you into this world."

"Brought me into it, and then threw me away," Kevin said, "me and you both. I bet you were glad I killed that bitch he left you for."

Kevin's eyes widened in shock when Sarah's palm whipped across his face. "Are you crazy? She was a human being. And I agreed to leave Wash. He never threw me out, and he never abandoned either me or you. He should never have told you he was your father."

"Sure he gave us all little half-ass slave jobs but he never owned up to why," Kevin said, "Just like you never did."

"What? Then how…?"

"I got into the Navy as soon as they'd take me, and the medical guys explained to me all about the operation I was too young to remember. A club foot. Just like Wash. I wondered about it the whole time I was in, even fantasizing about having a real dad and sharing his fortune. Then a training accident made it worse and worse, until I just wasn't combat ready and they gave me the medical discharge."

"And when you came back Wash put you on his payroll, doing pretty much nothing," Sarah said.

"You think playing personal assistant to that asshole was nothing?" Kevin asked. "He had me running all day. But now I had my suspicions because of the club foot thing. And the more I looked at him, the more I could see myself. So one day I just got him a new hairbrush. I sent the old one and some of my hair to a fellow I was still tight with in the Navy Medical Corps. It took a while, but he managed to get a DNA test done. That's how I found out that lying bastard was my own flesh and blood."

The last trace of disbelief faded from Sarah's expression and her face seemed to fall in on itself. After quickly scanning the available shoulders she spun and collapsed into Cindy's arms, sobbing hard.

"Okay, we understand that you're a psychopath," Cindy said through clenched teeth. "I see how you came up with this twisted plot to murder your way into your imagined inheritance. But still, he was your own flesh and blood. How could you kill your own father?"

"It was easy after I confronted him. I cornered him in the house and I demanded my birthright. He laughed in my face. He told me he had given me his cunning, and that was all he had for me. I had all I needed to get what I wanted myself, he said. Then he just brushed me off, me and my wife. The bastard sent me away, just like he sent my mother away as soon as he found out I was coming. He just turned his back on me. After that, it wasn't really about the money at all."

"Am I hearing this right?" Cindy asked, hugging Sarah tighter. "You telling me that you killed your father because of your wounded pride?"

Against the far wall, Orson Rissik gave a subtle nod, and two uniformed officers started dragging Kevin toward the door. But his eyes were still on Cindy.

"You just don't get it, do you bitch? That bastard denied me."

Hannibal shook his head. "Yeah, well maybe he understood what you had become." Then, as Kevin passed through the door,

Hannibal turned to Rissik. "I got to say, chief, I'm surprised you let that go on as long as you did."

Rissik shrugged. "Hey, I had my confession in front of a room full of witnesses. He wasn't going anywhere. And I guess I figured his mother deserved a real explanations, maybe a little closure."

Darryl looked at Rissik, his head cocked to one side. "You know, you all right for a cop. So, is my big brother going to the House of D in Fairfax where they put me and the boys?"

Rissik thought for a moment before allowing a small, sly smile to curl one side of his mouth. "Yes, I'm quite sure Mr. Larson, born Kevin Thomas, will be remanded to the Adult Detention Center. Now I'm not sure how the attorneys will feel about it, since you're going to testify against him in court, but I think I just might be able to arrange a little family reunion while you're all there."

## -22-

The ocean over the side of the catamaran was a blue that Hannibal had thought only existed in a Crayola box. Cindy had used the word azure and he assumed she was right. To him, it was just blue, but a blue that didn't exist in the real world, only in cartoons. A few minutes ago he had been in that cartoon world, diving deep into the limitless sea, able to see forever in every direction and able to go as deep as his lungs would allow before shooting to the surface to take another breath through a snorkel tube. Then he had dived deep to greet colorful, exotic fish and coral with his personal mermaid by his side.

He spit out the saltiness and dropped his mask on the deck. Behind him, Cindy laid a hand on his shoulder, three shades darker than usual, and for the hundredth time whispered, "Thank you."

"You deserve it and more," Hannibal said. "Besides, I'm having at least as much fun as you are so…"

"Don't spoil it," Cindy said. "Just let me appreciate my knight."

Saint Tropez was just a fishing village in the sense that Las Vegas is just a Western frontier town. To Hannibal it was like walking through a movie set but to Cindy it was Disney World in French. But the sand on the beach really had been white, the drinks had been strong, and their time on and in the water truly magical. And healing.

"I'm happy with you just enjoying a vacation with your man."

"A vacation?" Cindy dropped to the deck, pulling him down to sit with her staring out at the horizon. "Hannibal you haven't

198just brought me to wonderland. You saved my life. You know that don't you?"

"I think you're overstating a bit."

She punched his shoulder. "Don't you dare make it less than it is. Maybe you don't understand how important your work is to people. Maybe I didn't know until this week."

"You're talking of me closing the case?"

"You gave me closure by finding the man who killed my good friend. You allowed me to understand why someone would steal him away from me. You let me see exactly how and why I was not to blame, and that I wasn't a random victim. My world was spun into chaos, and you restored order."

Hannibal closed his eyes for a moment, just enjoying the feeling of his woman's arm around his shoulders. Could she be right? Was he some kind of knight in shining armor? No. Not a knight or a hero, he decided. He was just a sheepdog, sent there to protect the sheep in his charge from the wolves who wandered the world.

"Cindy, I love you, and I'm glad I was able to keep to our plans and bring you to the Riviera. The rest, well, it's just what I do babe. So, how about you just thank me for the trip?"

Cindy's smooth skin glowed in the sun. Hannibal slid a hand into her hair, covered her mouth with his own, and accepted his fair and just reward.

# Author's Bio

Austin S. Camacho is the author of the Hannibal Jones Mystery Series and the Stark and O'Brien adventure series. His short stories have been featured in four anthologies from Wolfmont Press, including Dying in a Winter Wonderland – an Independent Mystery Booksellers Association Top Ten Bestseller for 2008 - and he is featured in the Edgar nominated African American Mystery Writers: A Historical and Thematic Study by Frankie Y. Bailey.

He is also a communications specialist for the Department of Defense. America's military people know him because for more than a decade his radio and television news reports were transmitted to them daily on the American Forces Network.

Camacho was born in New York City but grew up in Saratoga Springs, New York. He majored in psychology at Union College in Schenectady, New York. After three years, he enlisted in the Army as a weapons repairman but soon moved on to being a broadcast journalist.

During his years as a soldier, Camacho lived in Missouri, California, Maryland, Georgia and Belgium. He also spent a couple of intense weeks in Israel during Desert Storm, covering the action with the Patriot missile crews and capturing scud showers on video tape. In his spare time, he began writing adventure and mystery stories set in some of the exotic places he'd visited.

After leaving the Army he continued to write military news for the Defense Department as a civilian. Today he handles media relations for DoD and writes articles for military newspapers and magazines. Camacho is a past president of the Maryland Writers Association, past Vice President of the Virginia Writers Club, and is an active member of Mystery Writers of America, International Thriller Writers and Sisters in Crime.

The Camacho family has settled in Upper Marlboro, MD with Princess the Wonder Cat and their dog, The Mighty Mocha.